DARK
SPELL

DARK
SPELL

DARKHAVEN SAGA: BOOK FOUR

DANIELLE ROSE

WATERHOUSE PRESS

For Heather—
because you inspire me to write a more
selfless, beautiful, and strong version of Ava.
Never dull your shine.

ONE

The world is silent. The chill in my bones and ache in my muscles will not relinquish their hold over me, no matter how desperately I try to shake away the feeling. Relief is always out of my grasp.

I stare at my hands, noticing how much I have aged in these few short months. My skin, no longer smooth or cool or pale, is dry and cracked, tainted by nights of neglect. Before, I did not have to worry about the mundane.

But I do now.

I feel its disappearance. There is a hole in my gut, and it screams at me. It is dark and dank and hollow within my core, and it stares me down, angry with my choices but conflicted by my lack of emotions. It is just as confused as I am.

The darkness within my body wants me to react, but I cannot. The world is spinning, moving forward in time, while I am desperate to latch on to something safe and familiar. I feel as though I will be lost in this moment forever, never quite finding my way home and always aware that I am without hope of ever being found.

Only moments ago, I was grounded between two worlds, yet a resident of neither. Now, I am slipping away, floating into the darkness, releasing my hold over the physical plane and entering the abyss. The world moves below me, and I watch it from where I am perched. I try to reach for the girl I once was, but she moves away at the perfect moment for me to grab on to her.

I sit in a chair. I do not know how I got inside the house, but somehow, I am here. I am no longer lying on the grass, looking at the sun. I no longer feel the burn in my eyes from staring at it for far too long. I am no longer blinded by my desire to watch as the world is bathed in light.

I am at a table. I lean back in my chair, moving so mechanically I have to wonder if I am even alive at all. Maybe this is a dream, and I will wake soon. But I know it is a lie my mind is telling me.

I look around the room but only as far as my eyes can see.

I do not turn my head to see more.

I do not inhale deeply for familiar scents.

I do not listen for noticeable sounds.

I do not taste the morning dew that lingers in the air.

I do not feel the earth calling to me.

Cut off from my senses, I am empty, hollow, dead.

"Ava, *¿puedes escucharme?*" *Mamá* asks.

I do not respond. I hear her voice. I know my mother is asking if I can hear her, and part of me does. The part that is still encased within my mortal coil responds to her voice, to her nearness, to her familiarity. I know she is beside me, crouching to look into my eyes. I see her worry lines, her tired eyes. She smells like sage. When I look at her, I see the fear in her eyes, hear it in her voice.

But the part of me that truly lived, the part that really experienced this world and all it could offer me, does not hear her. Because it *can't* hear anymore.

The vampire is dead.

I know the exact moment it was ripped from my soul, tearing through flesh, leaving a ragged, haggard mess in its wake. What remains is an emptiness, and it threatens to swallow me whole.

When I look into the dark pit, I suck in a sharp, steely breath, and I almost want it to devour me. I am desperate to escape this world, even if my only escape is a prison far worse than the one I am held in now.

The dark spell Mamá performed severed the witch from the vampire. No longer a hybrid, I feel as though I am neither. With the vampire gone, the witch is supposed to remain, but does she? I do not feel the way I used to. In fact, I do not feel like a witch *or* a mortal. I do not even feel *alive*. I am dead, and that sensation blankets me, embracing each curve in darkness. The seclusion is suffocating.

"Ava, answer your elder," someone says, trying to break my silence.

Does she not understand that I *want* to respond? I *want* to feel normal and answer and be my usual witty self. But I cannot. My silence is not laced with spite or malicious intentions. I just. can't. answer.

She clears her throat, and I know her voice. It is *Abuela*, my grandmother. She is the high priestess of this coven, and *she* is the reason I am like this. When she severed my better half, she linked my soul to my mother's. Even now, I feel Mamá's aura inside me. I feel her more prominently in my very soul than I feel my own essence.

It strikes me suddenly, and I am overwhelmed by the thought that *pain* might be the only thing left for me. What kind of life is that? Why would Mamá risk such magic? And how can she do this to a loved one?

When I think of my mother, I see only evil. That darkness and its promise are silencing my fears. It speaks to me, telling me I will never be alone, not anymore, even when I want so desperately to shake free from its chains. I do not want to be tied to her. This invisible connection is forming a noose around my neck, and it is tightening around my throat so I cannot speak, cannot scream, cannot plead with my captors for my freedom.

But even if I could, I know my mother would not grant it. They will never allow me to return to the vampires, and even more so, they will not risk temptation. But what does that mean? Will I forever remain within these walls, a prisoner in my own childhood home? Am I to live here? To die here? I imagine my mother intends to never let me go. This spell ensures my life is now in her hands.

I would give anything to be a hybrid again. I want to connect to the earth. I want to feel the wind against my skin as I run through the forest. I want to smell the rain and hear the slithering of worms in the soil. I want to touch the new fallen snow and feel more than its crisp bite at my fingertips.

The darkness shades everything in gloom, and I am drowning. I cannot move, cannot think, cannot speak, but I am well aware that I am sinking further into black quicksand. I feel the grains between my fingers and toes. The grit coats my legs and cakes around the curves of my chest. It is heavy against my lungs, and I want to scream. I want to shout at the witches and curse them for what they have done.

But I do not. I cannot. Like my mind, my muscles are numb, my voice mute. When I close my eyes, I see flashes of crimson irises and waves of blood. When I open them, I see only a loveless house, inhabited by heartless strangers.

A single tear escapes my lid, sliding down the sharp slope of my bones until it splashes on my chest. It seeps through my shirt, but I do not feel the dampness. I watch its slow progression, completely immobilized and dazed.

When I scan the room again, searching for something familiar, something *safe*, I spot Will. He walks into the house from the sliding doors that lead to the backyard. The witches usher him inside, seating him across from me. He follows their lead, silent and compliant.

He does not look at me. His eyes, no longer crimson, are dark and moody. They are deep brown or maybe blue. Sitting a few feet away, I cannot tell. I blink several times, trying to clear my vision, but it is no use. I cannot see him any clearer. The color of his eyes remains a mystery, but one thing is certain: he is not a vampire anymore.

His hair is messy and damp. His face is scratched and bloodstained. His nose is bleeding, and a single line drips down his chin. His lips are cracked and dry. When the glass doors open, sending a rush of wind throughout the house, he and I both shiver from the icy breeze. The witches, dressed to withstand the sharp lashings winter bestows upon Darkhaven, do not react to the cold.

Liv is standing near Will, but she is looking at me. I wonder how I look to her. Do I look as different as I feel? Or will the witches expect me to be the girl they once knew?

But I know I am not her. Not anymore. The Ava they mourn died so long ago, I feel as though I never knew her at all. I am not confident they knew her either. I like who I became after my transition. I was strong and selfless, loved and respected. And I had friends, *family*, who would die for me.

I yearn to see Jasik again. I think Mamá's final cruel joke

when she left me a shell of the girl I once was, was that she stole all senses save for one: my ability to feel pain. I ache for my sire from my heart to the depths of my soul. The truth that I abandoned him to save these people, who would no sooner burn me at the stake, does not sit easy with me.

I feel their betrayal in my bones, and it stings like the summer Mamá doused my fresh cuts in lemon juice, praising the tart fruit's healing properties. I did not heal any faster, but the pain from cutting my hand eased after I had something new to focus on: the tart bite of deception.

"Perhaps they should rest," Liv says, her voice soft and far too quiet for the girl who helped plan my demise. What happened to the brazen fire witch who threatened to set me aflame? Was she sent into the same bleak hole as the vampire who once inhabited my body?

I glance at her, and I see her agony. She hates herself for what she's done to me, but I cannot help believing she only feels regret because I am mortal again. If I were still a vampire, would she care? If I died instead of being reborn, would she mourn me? I remember the way she looked only an hour ago. She had such anger, such hatred in her eyes, so I do not think she would. Everything about her is fake.

Mamá guides me from the kitchen to the hallway. From the hallway, she leads me upstairs to my bedroom. Gently, she places me on the bed, tucks me in beneath the covers, and kisses my forehead.

"I know this is difficult for you, *mija*," she says. "But trust that I am doing what is best for you."

I squeeze my eyes shut, not wanting to look into hers any longer. I hate that they look like hers now.

When she leaves, she turns off the light and closes my bedroom door.

I stare at the ceiling. The thick curtains are drawn, but sunlight shines through the edges. Even with these strips of light, I cannot see the room. It is so dim that I find myself drifting off, with nothing but the steady clicks of a nearby clock to guide me into the abyss.

When I wake, the sun is gone, and the moon does not speak to me. I touch the window, letting the rush of cold slither from my fingertips to my spine. Goose bumps form, and I wrap my arms around myself to keep out the chill.

Ignoring a note on my bedside table to wash and dress, I stare at my old bedroom. Mamá kept it the same, and as I pace the floor, I shuffle through the items I could not take the first time I was ousted from my childhood home.

Pictures are still stacked in a pile on the floor. My desk is still cluttered, gathering dust like the rest of my potential. When I reach my dresser, my breath catches in my throat. Sitting atop the scratched wood surface is a plain black box. It is rectangular and sleek. I run my fingertips along the edges and gnaw on my lower lip, praying this is not part of my mother's cruel game.

I open the box, letting the lid fall back as I stare inside. Sleek, matte gray with a shiny silver tip, my stake glistens at me. Etched with runes and doused in magic, it yearns to be used. It used to call to me, but now, I hear nothing. I *feel* nothing.

As I tease the metal with my fingers, I find myself wondering if this was Mamá's plan all along. Did she hope I would leave this behind one day? Did she intend to reintroduce us after performing her dark spell? Did she plan for this to be a peace offering or a welcome-home gift?

I grasp the weapon and curl my fingers around its girth. Sniffling, I remember when *Papá* gave this to me. As Abuela's son, he was supposed to take over leadership of the coven, and then it was to go to me. His death meant he would be bypassed, and for as long as I can remember, I felt obligated to prove myself to my grandmother. I never wanted to be a leader. I wanted to be a savior. I wanted to protect the humans and witches of Darkhaven from vampires. Only after I transitioned did I learn about the witches' dishonesty.

I glance at my weapon as it rolls against my palm. It feels... different. Off somehow. Or maybe it is me. Either I have lost my power and my connection to the earth, or my stake has, and honestly, I am not sure I want to know which.

I wipe my nose and slide my stake into my jacket's inner pocket. This is where I have kept it for years. I used this very weapon in my quest to rid the world of evil—or what I *thought* to be evil. Later, when I learned only rogue vampires have bad intentions, I tried to explain my discovery to the witches. They did not believe me, listen, or care about my findings. They just wanted vampires dead.

I try to withdraw my stake quickly, seamlessly, and I stumble over the motions. I lose grip of it, and it tumbles to the floor. It smacks against the hardwood, clanking viciously until it rolls to a stop. I scoop it up so quickly, I nearly trip over my feet. I lean against the bed frame and securely tuck my weapon back into my pocket.

My heart is pounding in my chest. I am so fearful the stake was placed there by accident and that the witches are going to make me give it back. But I do not want to. I may be surrounded by his pictures hanging from frames on the walls in every room of this house, but once I break free from this prison, my stake and my cross necklace are all I will have left of Papá.

I thumb the necklace at my chest, finding the familiar, smooth metal to be soothing, but still, something seems different. Everything about how I experience the world has changed. I do not feel comfortable in my own skin or my childhood home or even in Darkhaven. And I am terrified of what the witches will do next.

I cross over to the window and pull back the curtain. The moon is high in the sky, cascading light over the small village. I run my tongue over my teeth, where there once were fangs, and sigh. With one quick, sharp exhalation, I exit my bedroom and venture downstairs. If I want to escape this hell, I need to show the witches I am one of them again. Maybe they will let down their guard long enough for me to find my way back to the vampires.

"Good evening, Ava," Abuela says. She stands as I walk into the living room.

I nod at her and glance around the room, searching for Will. When the witches have gone to bed, I plan to make my escape, and I bet he will want to come with me. When I do not find him right away, I frown. Where could he have gone? Better yet, what have the witches done to him?

"Where is Will?" I ask, my tone much more forceful than I intended. Internally, I chastise myself. This is the first time I have spoken to them since being cursed, and my concern is for Will, not the others. Even though I know this will not win me any favors, I cannot help myself. I *must* find him.

Abuela narrows her gaze at me, sensing my frustration with our situation. I do not hide the fact that I fear for his safety, and this upsets my grandmother.

"Why don't you take a seat," my grandmother says. "We have much to discuss."

"I do not want to sit. I want to find Will. Where is he?"

I sound like an unruly child, but I do not care. I will not relent until he and I are reunited, even if that means facing the worst the witches can throw at me. I brace for impact, resigning myself to what is sure to be misery and pain.

"Ava, *mija, por favor siéntate*," Mamá says.

I did not hear her approach. She crosses the room and reaches my side. With her guiding hand, she ushers me to a seat in the only open chair. Her subtle direction but firm tone is all I need to succumb to her desire.

"Where is Will, Mamá?" I ask, hoping I can play on her guilt. I speak softly, kindly.

"Él está por allá. He is with Liv," Mamá says. She glances over my shoulder, her eyes guiding me to where I cannot see.

I frown and follow her gaze. He is sitting at the dining table, in the very seat he was ushered to hours ago.

"Has he been there this whole time?" I ask, confused.

Mamá nods.

My heart sinks, knowing how exhausted he must feel, and a small part of me is afraid his exhaustion will be his weakness. If we plan to escape a coven of witches, I need him at his full strength. The moment we get outdoors, we will have to run, and the woods will not be kind to us.

I stand to aid him, but Mamá's hand at my shoulder stops me. When I look into her eyes, I see something there. I lose myself in her gaze, my mind swirling around this quiet void.

"You need to calm down, Ava," she says.

Her voice is cool, quiet, and it entrances me. I nod, feeling suddenly at ease.

"Yes, Mamá," I say.

I blink, and I am seated again, but the moment she looks away, breaking our gaze, that feeling is gone. Fear rises in my chest, settling in my heart. It pricks at me, puncturing flesh until I bubble with worry. I want to shriek, to get her essence out of my body, for now I understand the link and its purpose. Mamá will use her power over me to keep me in line, to do her bidding and follow her commands.

Before I can respond to this invasion of self-control, Liv rushes in, dashing to Abuela's side quickly. She whispers something in her ear, and I watch as the color drains from her face and her eyes become fiery pits.

When Abuela catches my attention, she smiles at me. It does not meet her eyes. The sinister glare she is giving me forces me to look away. I hate that I am a descendant of her blood. I do not want to be privy to such innate evil.

"What is it?" Mamá asks, frowning. Her voice is laced with concern.

"It seems we have visitors," Abuela says, her gaze fluttering from my mother to me. "Come. We shall greet them together."

When we step outside, I am assaulted by the cold night air. Lip quivering, I shiver, wrapping my arms around my body. The others are wrapped in thick winter garments, but Will and I are dressed in the clothes we were wearing last night. The outfits offered plenty of protection for a vampire, but for witches, we are welcoming hypothermia.

Intentionally keeping Will and me back, the witches are blocking our sight. We cannot see our visitors, and the rush of wind blowing through the trees makes it hard to hear. My teeth clatter together as a gust works its way through my loose T-shirt.

I close my eyes, focusing intently on the conversation being had mere feet from me. *Why* is it so hard to hear, so hard to focus? I glance at Will, wondering if he is struggling with our transition as much as I am.

"Bring them forward," Abuela shouts loud enough for everyone to hear. Someone grabs on to my arm, squeezing it tightly. I gasp in response as pain rushes down my limb as my attacker digs in her nails. I wince, grinding my teeth as I stumble away from Will.

I am shuffling forward, moving so quickly, I trip over my feet. When I reach the forefront of the witches who surrounded us, I understand why Abuela had such malicious intentions. This is her moment to shine, her pride in what she has done to me, her only grandchild. This is the moment she can watch the repercussions unfold, for I am no longer a vampire.

Even when I was sacrificing everything to aid the witches, I still chose my new allies over my former coven. And now, the vampires can witness the birth of something else. Will they accept me as I am now? Abuela must not believe so. She wants to witness their rejection.

I make eye contact with Jasik, and the world slows. All I hear is my heart in my head, and all I feel is the burning desire to be wrapped in his arms. I want his love, his devotion, his protection. I want *him*. I want the life I lost, the life I took for granted.

"Jasik," I whisper.

He frowns, brow furrowing in his confusion. No doubt, he senses something is...off. I probably do not smell the same or sound the same or look the same. Not anymore. My irises are not crimson, my skin is not perfect and smooth, and I probably smell like heavenly meals on wheels.

He cocks his head, gaze scanning my frail frame like he does not quite recognize me, and I completely shatter. A pathetic screech escapes my lips as tears burn behind my eyes. In a desperate attempt to control my emotions, I bite my lip so hard, I break skin.

I smell nothing, taste nothing, but the immediate reaction from the vampires tells me *they* sense my change. Their eyes widen—from fear or wonder or curiosity, I will never know. But this is the moment they truly understand just how *different* I am now.

"Ava?" Jasik whispers, and I fear this is the last time I will ever hear my name grace his lips, so I cherish the moment. I close my eyes, playing the sound of his voice over and over again in my mind, imprinting the way he looked at me before I became...*this*.

"What have they done to you?" Hikari says, seething.

Her disgust is evident in her tone. I do not need to see it on her face, but I look anyway and see shock strewn across her face. The look she gives me is just plain...ugly.

I hiccup through my breaths, silently pleading with the vampires to accept me. I cannot stay here, and I beg them not to leave me with the witches, but words never escape my lips.

"She is one of us now," Mamá says as she steps forward. "A witch, reborn."

"As you can see, there is nothing for you here," Abuela says.

Everything happens in slow motion. My vision is spinning as I fall to my knees. The impact of the frozen earth penetrating my jeans sends a rush of pain jolting through my legs. I slump forward, catching my fall with my palms. My flesh is numbed by the frosty ground.

I glance up, meeting Jasik's confused gaze, and pretend the look he is giving me does not completely destroy my heart. I want him to see me as I was when I was *his*. He looked at me with devotion and longing, like he could not wait to unravel my layers, uncovering my personal quirks. But that look is gone, and I cannot bear what remains.

"Please, it is me. I am still *me*," I whisper, but my voice is so soft and the wind is so strong, I fear no one hears me. I have to wonder if I ever even spoke at all. Maybe this is all in my mind. Maybe I am asleep and my imagination is overtaking my sanity.

But I know that is a fool's wish.

I sit back, resting my bottom against my sloppy, wet heels. Jasik takes one cautionary step toward me, but Malik stops him. With a firm hand wrapped around his younger brother's shoulder, he silently warns him of impending danger. He fears this could be a trap, and for all I know, it is.

Jasik nudges his brother's hand off him and takes another step forward, never breaking my gaze as he closes in on me.

He reaches for me, moving far too quickly for my mortal eyes to bear. He flashes before me, and I close my eyes, welcoming the inevitable.

I know I should be scared. If I am a witch, then I am mortal. Vampires feed on the living. I am bleeding and scared and weak. I am the perfect prey.

But I do not fear for my life, because even a death at the hands of vampires is a fate far better than what the witches plan to bestow upon me.

TWO

Jasik crouches beside me. I stare at the ground, hair shielding my vision from seeing the uncertainty in his eyes. I cannot bear to look at his crimson irises any longer. I hate that he must see me like this—so weak, so unlike the girl he saved all those months ago. I imagine I look nothing like her now.

My hair is dull, frizzy, and lifeless. My skin is imperfect and dry. My eyes are likely murky, a muddled brown color so drastically different from their usual crimson glow. I squeeze my eyes shut so he does not have to look at them, wishing I could get the vision of me out of my mind. Even I do not want to look at the mess I have become, so why would he want to see me this way?

I feel his fingertips grace my skin, and I hold my breath. After several seconds pass, I choke out a gasp. I open my eyes to find him tucking loose strands of my hair behind my ear. He moves so calmly, so quietly, and he touches me so softly, as if he is afraid he might harm me with just his fingers. I imagine I probably do look that weak to him. After all, I am broken, feeling shattered beyond repair. I feel lifeless and frail. The fire within me that attracted him to me has been smothered, and all that is left is its smoky remains.

Gnawing on my lower lip, I glance up at him. Even when he kneels beside me, he towers over my cowering frame. I flinch when he moves quickly, and I watch him frown, his eyes pained by my reaction to him. I know he would not hurt me, and I hate that I made him think I might worry about that now.

"Ava..." Jasik whispers my name; it almost sounds like a plea. He sounds as broken as I feel.

"For Christ's sake, what have they done to you?" Hikari says. I steal a glance, finding her closing the space between her and Will. She crouches down, resting her hand on his back. Her black pixie hair is spiky and shiny. The moonlight reflects off each pointed strand, betraying her overuse of product. She looks greasy, but something about seeing her this way reminds me of life at the manor.

"We need to get out of here," Jeremiah says. My gaze finds his, and I see sorrow in his eyes. Why is he unhappy? Does he wish he would have aided me last night? I shake my head, hoping he can understand my meaning. The only reason Will and I survived is because we are—*were*—hybrids. Jeremiah would have died last night if he attempted to help me. And I could not live with myself if we lost him too.

Jeremiah tears his gaze from mine and remains focused on the witches. His hands are balled into fists at his sides. His knuckles are ashy, and his usually deep, dark skin is coated in a fine dust from winter's cruel, dry weather. I scratch at my hands, feeling my own desire for a rich lather.

I begin to shake, the reality of the bitter cold sinking in. I think Jasik mistakes my shudder as something more, because he pulls away from me again. The separation between the two of us is almost too much to bear. My body aches for him, and I am desperate to hold him close. I want to feel safe again. I want to feel strong.

I look at him, but he is looking at something in the distance. I take this moment to consider how these events have altered the course of his life too. Will he ever feel comfortable around me? When I look from vampire to vampire, they all seem uneasy. I assume it is because they are surrounded by their enemy, but what if it is something more? What if things never return to normal?

Malik, Jasik's biological older brother, is watching the witches. He does not look at me. As my trainer, I wonder if I have upset him. *This* is why he pushes me to the very edge of my limits and then watches as I fall off the cliff. He wanted me to be strong enough to survive any attack, and I did the exact opposite. I walked into the witches' trap with a smile on my face and a song in my heart. I was too stubborn and hardheaded to see what the vampires saw the moment they met my coven.

Malik has his dagger drawn, and he traces circles in the leather-strapped handle. His gaze lands on each witch, and then he repeats the process. He never lingers for too long on any one witch. Always the warrior, I know he is cultivating a plan right now. I am just not sure if saving Will and me is part of it.

The only vampire I cannot bear to look at is Jasik, my sire. I hate that his eyes reveal his disappointment. I fear the harshness of his words and cannot handle another betrayal, so I do not even ask him to take me with him.

I squeeze my eyes shut so tightly, I draw tears. With one slow, overdrawn exhalation, I open them and meet my sire's gaze. His crimson irises sparkle in the darkness. Should I be scared of being so close to a vampire? I haven't any way to protect myself if he chooses to lash out.

"My Ava," Jasik whispers. His thumb traces the edge of

my jaw, lingering at the center of my chin. He presses slightly, firmly into the divot there, and smiles at me.

I fall against him, relishing in the feeling of being so near to something so safe, so loving, so true. I burrow my face in the crevice of his neck and pretend we are not at Mamá's house. We are not surrounded by witches. We are not on the brink of yet another war.

We are in the manor. We are home. We are *safe*.

"Time to go now, love," Jasik says, and I fall deeper into the depths. He smells like mint and the winter breeze and... *blood*.

I open my eyes, inhaling deeply as I take in his essence. I grab on to him tighter, wanting to take in his scent. He holds me, cocooning my body in his embrace, as if his arms alone could shield me from my hellish life.

"Step away from her," Mamá says. I did not hear her approach us, but I do sense her anger. Like Abuela, she wanted me to suffer. She wanted to witness the vampires abandon me just as the witches had.

Jasik tenses, his arms turning to impenetrable shields of pure steely strength. I do not fear for Mamá's safety, but I know she should.

Jasik releases me and stands. I follow suit, facing him as he stares down at the witches. They attempt to corner the vampires, to encircle them in some magical binding. I know nothing would make the witches happier than allowing me to watch the vampires die a brutal, fiery death, but the vampires are far too smart for their feeble tricks.

"We are leaving," Jasik says.

My sire slides his hand against mine, interlocking his fingers with my own. His skin is cold, and I wonder how I feel to him. Do I feel the same? Jasik does not acknowledge the changes in my body, but I certainly do.

I glance at Will, who is being aided by Hikari. While her back is turned, Jeremiah is watching the witches carefully. Prepared to defend his pack, he is a hungry wolf ready to strike. Will falls against Hikari's much smaller frame and lets her guide him away from the witches. She is able to successfully retrieve him because their attention is focused solely on *me*.

"You are not taking her anywhere," Mamá says.

Jasik's eyes narrow, his grip tightening around my hand. If the witches pooled their air magic and attempted to yank me free from his grasp, I fear I would be dismembered right before his eyes.

I glance over my shoulder and say, "*Por favor, Mamá, no hagas esto más difícil de lo que tiene que ser.*"

I beg her not to make this harder than it has to be. There does not need to be bloodshed. No one has to die today. The witches won. I am no longer a hybrid. Now they can let me go.

"*Cállate, niña,*" Abuela says. "*Perteneces con nosotros.*"

I swallow the knot that forms and listen to her admonition. *I belong with them.*

What she really means to say is I belong *to* them.

"You are never going to let me go," I whisper. "I will never be free."

Jasik soothes my fears with the touch of his hand. He caresses my skin with his thumb, drawing circular motions to root me in place. I look to him, and silently, he tells me everything will be okay. And I believe him.

With one final glance, he tears his gaze from mine and looks at the witches. The outrage I see in them makes me shudder. I cower beside him, terrified of what he will do next.

My sire will stop at nothing to protect me—this I know to be true.

"Let me make myself very clear. I will kill *everyone* you have ever met if that is what I must do to save her," Jasik warns. "Either you will die tonight or you will live tomorrow. The choice is yours, but you will not keep her here any longer."

I gasp, shocked by his admission, by his threat. The vampires are outnumbered, but they offer a clear warning. Until now, they have obeyed my request to maintain peace. They have only used the strength and skill necessary to survive battles, but they have not maliciously targeted my former coven. In spite of everything the witches have done to them, to *me*, the vampires have allowed some semblance of peace simply because I requested it. Now that I do not, and now that I fear for my very life, they will not yield.

I should feel sad. I should be outraged by the mere thought of losing my family. I should be saddened by Mamá's impending death. But I am not. She created this new, desensitized version of her daughter when she muted my better half. She made me numb to most feelings, and that includes the part that would mourn her demise.

"Do you truly believe you can overpower a coven?" Abuela asks. "Are you that sure of yourselves?"

"We have been training for these very moments far longer than you have been alive, lady," Jeremiah says.

"I think a better question is if you think *you* are strong enough to beat *us*," Hikari says.

Will is standing beside her, holding himself upright. He eyes me cautiously, a silent warning. We are weakened by their spell, but we are not powerless. We might not be able to call upon magic—*yet*—but we know basic tactics. We can beat them. We just have to be smarter. And I like to think that we are.

Malik passes Will a weapon. The dagger is sleek, with a slightly curved blade, either intentional or from years of battle. The shiny silver betrays the countless hours he has sharpened its edge. As Will takes the weapon from Malik, I see the worn leather handle, dulled by years of being held by a strong, defiant hand.

I remember my stake. It is snug within the inner breast pocket of my military-style jacket. Silently, I thank Mamá for returning it to me, but a pit forms in my gut when I think of how I plan to use it.

Years of fighting has granted me expert precision. I can slice the pointed tip through the air with such velocity, it will penetrate the thick sternum of muscle and bone to pierce the heart. This is an awful way to kill a witch. I will be forced to watch her fear, her pain, and her agonizing death. Why can't witches die as quickly as a vampire? Their painless combustion from form to ash seems unfair.

"If you think we are not prepared for this fight, then you are sadly mistaken," Abuela says.

She eyes another witch. The shift in her vision is so brief, I almost miss it. I am sure the vampires notice the break in her focus, but quickly, her gaze lands back on them. I have seen this same look in her eyes many times before. Except, back then, I was never the target of her wrath.

Everything happens so quickly, I do not have enough time to warn the others. My grandmother nods, and a blast of unified elemental witches assaults my frail frame.

My hand is ripped from Jasik's, and I am flying. I soar through the air, body limp, as I allow the elements to carry me where they wish, for there is no point in fighting. The vampires withstand the brunt of the attack, using their superior strength to fight against the torrential waves of magic and power.

My allies skid backward but remain upright until the blasts of energy cease, and the witches clasp hands. We are centerfold now, encircled by my coven, awaiting the best they can throw at us.

I slump against the ground, a jagged edge of something sharp stabbing me in the back as I fall into a heap of brush. Something crunches beneath my weight—perhaps something icy or maybe a pointed branch—and the sound radiates all around me. Instantly, I am overcome with fear. I begin my mental check.

Am I okay?

Have I broken something?

Can I stand?

Can I *fight*?

My legs ache, my spine tingling when I try to move. I try to calm my breathing, taking slow, long, intentional inhalations until the fire in my gut subsides. It feels like hours pass as I wait for the strength to stand, but I know it has been only seconds.

I hear their fight erupting all around me.

As I lie on the ground, coated in the remnants of earth's most brutal season, I see flashes of light and hear the painful cries of dying witches. I do not hear the vampires crying out, but that does not mean they are not in trouble. The moment a stake penetrates the heart, they begin their descent to death. It is quick and often silent. So even though I do not hear my friends crying out for help, that does not mean they are fighting. That does not mean they are still *alive*.

I roll onto my side and force myself into a seated position.

My hands are caked with ice and mulch. I brush my palms on my jeans as I scan my surroundings.

The world around me has exploded in violence. The witches team up in groups of four—one representing each physical element—to fight against each vampire. This is keeping Malik, Hikari, and Jeremiah busy, but Jasik is making his way to me. He rushes to my side, blood splattered across his face. I do not ask whose blood as he ushers me to my feet. I lean against him and wince as a sharp pain radiates through my leg.

"You are hurt," Jasik says.

I shake my head. "I am fine. Go. Help the others."

He frowns at me, his eyes in disbelief. "You do not really expect me to obey that order, do you?"

I smile, and for one brief second, it is just the two of us again, but that feeling is torn away from me the moment a sharp dagger of enhanced air magic rips through my sire's chest. His blood spews from his wound as he howls. It sprays onto my face, and I scream. The magic penetrates completely through his chest and shoots out through his sternum. I look away just in time, and the dagger of invisible energy slices across my cheek. It disappears into the forest, and Jasik falls to his knees beside me.

I drop to my knees, ignoring the stabbing pain in my throbbing leg. My body protests, warning me of my weakened state. I am wounded, but I do not care. Jasik is on the verge of death.

He slumps forward, breaking his fall with one outstretched arm. But it too yields, and he collapses to the ground, face pressed into the snow. His chest is heaving, his breath coming in powerful bursts, making the soft snow coating the earth flutter with each exhalation. If not for the bloodshed, I would say the woods look magical at this time of night. The moonlight makes everything glisten and sparkle, but just when I find it beautiful, I see streaks of crimson.

I cradle Jasik in my arms, rocking back and forth, telling him over and over again that he will be okay. I remind him it missed his heart, even if he already knows this information. If the witch did not miss, he would already be ash. I run my blood-caked fingers through his hair, and the dark-brown strands tangle in my grasp, sweeping around my fingers and clinging to my wet skin.

"You are going to be okay, Jasik," I whisper.

His head is rested against my lap, and I break his gaze to find help. The vampires are at war with the witches, evading attacks and blocking equally damning threats. Will is helping the others, taking every opportunity he can to outsmart his enemy.

I consider our depleted hybrid bodies. Together, can two halves make a whole? Can we combine our efforts to heal Jasik? Slowly, his body is healing itself, but he has not the time to wait for muscle to thread and bone to form. The moment one of these witches realizes he is badly injured, she will take it upon herself to end my sire's life once and for all. And that I will not allow.

I see Malik sparring with a witch I have never before seen, and I call for him, screaming his name with such agony, such desperation, such absolute terror, he halts. He freezes, if only for a second, and then uses the witch's distraction to end her life.

My trainer searches the grounds, seeking my voice, and when he finds me, he panics. I imagine what this must look like to him. I am sitting on the ground, covered in blood and sweat, and tears are streaming down my cheeks. Jasik, unmoving, is cradled in my arms.

I have never before seen such dread, such love and devotion in the eyes of a vampire who has trouble expressing his emotions. I fear for any witch who tries to block his path, for she will not survive his vengeance.

The moment someone does step between Malik and his brother, I squeeze my eyes shut. Because I know this witch. I remember her from before. She is older and powerful, and she was nice to me. She would sit with me for hours and talk about how pleasant Darkhaven used to be—before coven after coven moved into the village, claiming the town as their own. She spoke of a long-ago feud between the witches of Darkhaven before they all decided to simply share the town. They offer no such courtesy to the vampires.

When I open my eyes again, the witch I once knew is lying on the ground. Malik's hand is covered in blood, and he is stomping forward. His tunnel vision allows him to see nothing but us, nothing but his baby brother on the brink of death.

I do not look at her body anymore, because she does not move. Her chest is stained with crimson, her legs have buckled awkwardly, and her head is angled to face me. I do not know if her eyes are open. I do not know if she sees me aiding the vampires and not her. I do not bother looking—not because I do not want to see the accusations within her lifeless gaze, but because there is nothing I can do for her. The witches were warned, and still, they waged war. They should know better than anyone. In war, there are casualties.

"What happened?" Malik says. He is close enough for me to hear him, and he skids on his knees to a stop and assesses the damage.

"He is hurt!" I shout. "Help him!"

"Ava," Malik says, his voice calm. With his eyes, he tells me to calm down, to just breathe, and I know everything will be okay. Malik will not let his brother die. He would give his life to save Jasik's, and I pray it will not come to that.

With Malik's back turned on the witches, he lifts his gasping brother into his arms. Jasik's legs flop like jelly beside his older brother's, but he leans against him. With an arm wrapped around Malik's shoulders, Jasik trudges forward, wincing at the pain.

"Why isn't he healing?" I shout as I jump to my feet. My own throbbing leg protests, and I grind my teeth in response.

"This was a nearly deadly wound, Ava," Malik says, voice heavy. He grunts as he maintains his hold on his brother, who is offering little assistance as they escape the battlefield.

"But he will be okay?" I ask.

Malik does not respond, and I do not push for answers. Because as their backs are turned, another witch is rushing forward. Arms thrown out to her sides, she calls upon her element. I do not have to guess which element will aid her. She has the look—the confident gleam—of a fire witch. One spark, and Malik and Jasik are toast.

I block her attack, putting my body between her and them.

"No!" I shout. I throw out my arms, blocking her with merely my palms. It is a fool's errand, but I cannot back down.

She stops abruptly, furrowing her brow. She is confused, her gaze darting between the vampires and me. Malik glances over his shoulder and tries to move quicker. He is heading straight for the fence that separates Mamá's property and the woods beyond.

I fumble with my jacket but soon withdraw my stake. It

is a child's toy compared with a fire witch's magic, but it is all I have to protect them, to protect *me*.

"Move out of my way, girl," the witch says. She is another unknown face in a fury of violence. How has Mamá found so many witches willing to die for a cause they do not understand?

"That is not going to happen," I say. I straighten my back, standing taller, stronger. I may not be the strongest witch here, but I can certainly slow down this stranger enough to protect my friends.

"Do you really think you can stop me?" the girl says. "Look around, you are *all alone*."

"No, she is not alone," a voice says.

From behind, Will emerges. He stands beside me and grabs my hand. We interlock fingers, and I feel a rush of magic coursing between us. The witch falters. It is brief, but her momentary lapse is all I need to feel stronger. She is scared. Not of me. But of *us*. Together, maybe we really do form one pissed-off hybrid.

I see the moment the girl decides to call upon her magic. The instant she chooses life over death, something flashes behind her eyes. Her magic erupts within her, her eyes becoming a blazing inferno of raw energy. Her insides are boiling, and her skin bares that truth. In the dead of winter, on this cool night, she is sweating, her cheeks pink from the heat of magic. Not from fear but from power.

Unfortunately, someone else sees it too. The moment she raises her hand, wielding a burning fireball in her palm, a dagger aimed perfectly for her heart slices through the air. Unlike the witch who wielded an air dagger before her, this time it does not miss.

From clear across the yard, Jeremiah stands defiantly.

His now weaponless arm outstretched, he bares the truth of what just happened. He threw his only defense against the witches across the yard to protect *us*.

The light goes out in the witch's eyes, and I see the exact moment she dies. Her body falls to the ground, her chest an open, gushing wound. Emotionless, I withdraw the dagger, shivering as the prominent squish of warm flesh releases its hold on the blade.

Before I can consider my options, Will grabs the dagger and rushes toward Jeremiah. He holds it out before him, tripping over his feet as his mind moves too fast for his weakened legs. He tumbles to the ground, rolling against the wet grass. Towering over the clumsy witch, Jeremiah shakes his head at Will's pathetic attempt to return the vampire's dagger. He then helps him up, and together, they fight off another witch.

Someone calls to me, and I break my concentration. I scan the yard until I find Malik. He and Jasik are safely in the woods, and they call to me. I limp forward, leaving behind the massacre in favor of my two favorite vampires.

By the time I reach my ailing mate's side, all hell has broken loose. Hikari, Jeremiah, and Will are still battling the witches, but I focus on my sire and my trainer.

"We need to go," Malik says firmly.

"We cannot leave them!" I shout, turning away from my friends in order to rejoin the fight.

"Ava, stop! Think! You are in no shape to fight," Malik warns. He grabs my arm, holding me back.

"We cannot leave them behind!" I repeat, shocked he would even consider abandoning his fellow hunters.

"They are smart, Ava. They are strong. They will find their

way back to us," Malik assures me.

Silent and unbelieving, I do not respond, even when Malik releases me.

Torn between two worlds, I watch as Malik leads Jasik to safety. I turn and watch as my other friends desperately try to avoid the witches' attacks. They maneuver effortlessly around their enemies as if they truly have been preparing for this very fight.

With an ache in my heart I just cannot shake, I look at Will, who smiles. He nods, understanding my pain and frustration. As I take a step forward, he shakes his head, stopping me in my tracks. With one final glance, he grips the handle of his weapon tightly and returns to the fight.

The last time I see Will, he is rushing toward the witches, disappearing into a cloud of magic and a waterfall of blood.

THREE

The distance between us offers much-needed clarity. Finally free from Mamá's clutches, I feel in control of my own thoughts. It is as though her power over me weakens with every step I take.

Everything about the witches feels icky. Ever since they performed their spell, something dark has settled in my soul. I assume it is Mamá and her essence mingling with my own. No longer can I tell where I end and she begins. We have become one. Her burdens are now mine to bear.

Queasy from the thought, my stomach churns. I cross my arms, holding my chest as I trudge through the snow. I ignore the vampires, who offer strategically timed side glances my way. I am certain there is never a moment when no one is looking at me. I understand their concern—and curiosity—but I can *feel* their gazes, and it is making my heart race, head spin, and gut ache.

I squeeze my eyes shut, momentarily blinded by darkness. The snow falling splatters against my cheeks, and I shiver. My lip trembles, and I kick something with my foot. The tip of my boot is nudged beneath something solid, and I am falling forward before I even have time to open my eyes.

Jasik catches me. He reaches out, and I grab on to him, nearly pulling him down with me. We stop walking, and I settle into his comfortable gaze. He smiles at me, and his eyes soften. But I see their pain. The agony that burns within him is not just because he nearly died. His body is already healing, even if he is still too weak to battle.

The turmoil coursing through his veins, turning him to ice, is because of everything I have done. Ever since the vampires welcomed me into their nest, I have made mistake after mistake. They have risked their lives for me, for my incessant need to end a pointless feud. And while I still do believe the war between the witches and vampires is absurd, never again will I risk our lives to save theirs.

From this moment on, the witches are on their own, and I will reserve my strength to protect my new family—the vampires.

My heart burns when I think about Will. He is still with them, fighting my cause. Even if I am no longer a hybrid and have no use for his knowledge, I still miss his friendship. In just over a day's time, Will managed to worm his way into my heart. He was nice to me during a time I did not have many allies, and even though he did not know Liv or recognize her betrayal, he still tried to save her. He did it for me.

"Do you think the others..."

I trail off, not wanting to ask my question aloud. I do not want to think it in my head either. I scratch at my scalp, shaking as I try to work harmful images from my mind. It is times like these that I hate my overactive imagination.

"They will be fine," Jasik says, answering my unasked question.

I nod, swallowing the knot in my burning throat, and exhale slowly. I try to clear my thoughts and focus instead on what is happening here, now, but my mind keeps wandering back to our comrades.

I do not know much about Will's fighting style, but even as a mortal, he must be a threat to the witches. I assume he has hunted vampires before, and he clearly knows how to fight. He outmaneuvered the witches in the forest, and he will do it again tonight. I just have to have faith in him.

Jeremiah is resourceful. In the short amount of time I have known him, he always brings new and unique methods to each battle. It keeps his enemies on their toes, making him a real asset when we are hunting.

I know Hikari is an experienced fighter. Not considering Jasik or Malik, she is the strongest hunter Amicia sired. I often forget how powerful she is, because she is much shorter and a great deal smaller than even me. She has a petite frame, which often means her enemies misjudge her. I know I have. She uses her size and perceived threat level to her advantage often.

If Malik did not believe they could fend for themselves, he would not have abandoned them. He would have separated Jasik from the witches and gone back for the others. I am sure of this. Malik has strong bonds to his family, and he would never leave them behind if he thought they were in real danger.

We are close to the manor. We have a short hike remaining until we greet Amicia and the other vampires. Attempting to foresee her reaction to what has happened is more than enough to occupy my mind.

The last time I saw her, I spoke in anger. I was upset with the blood oath she forced upon me and what that meant for my freedom. She stole my ability to think for myself, to react in my natural ways. Now, I laugh at the anger I felt. I was quick to judge, not even considering my dark promise with Amicia would be the least of my problems. Come daybreak, I was severed from the very part of me that made me special, and now, I am linked to the spiteful, malicious woman who bore me.

Mamá gave me my life's blood, and in just as quick and natural of a decision, she tried to take it away. I wonder if there was a time she ever truly loved me.

I limp over a mound of snow, sinking into its depths. Beneath its pearlescent sheen, it hides layers of deception. Something crunches beneath my weight, and I assume I am walking over many years of brush.

Using a nearby tree to pull my legs free, I trample over the hump, landing in a heap on the other side. My ankles burn when the soles of my boots land firmly on the ground, and I rub my hands together to remove the grit and dead bark. Chest heaving from overexertion, I wipe the sweat that dribbles at the peak of my forehead.

Only then do I notice the vampires. They are watching me, concerned, but I try not to absorb their worry. The last thing I need right now is to fear how weak I have become.

The rest of the way, I gnaw on my lip and think about what has happened in my life over the past several months. I was destined to lead my coven, becoming the next high priestess in a long line of witches devoted to the cause. Their mission: to rid the world of vampires.

Then I became one, and ever since, I have been trying to piece together my upbringing. The witches dislike what I became so much, they risked my life to sever the darkness from my soul.

I cannot help but wonder what would have happened if the spell failed. I would have died, I know that, but what would have happened to Mamá? Would she have perished beside me? We are linked now, but I still do not fully understand what that means. My puzzle is only half-finished, and though I strive to put it together, I only have some of the pieces. What irks me is that Mamá does not need the ones I have to see the picture clearly, because she has the image this jigsaw puzzle becomes. And that makes her far too great a threat.

I exhale sharply and replay the spell in my mind. Using an ancient curse, the witches risked dark magic to bind Mamá's soul to mine. Based on their altar offerings, they used the power of the sun to harness enough energy to link us. In doing so, they have broken the sacred oath we follow to respect and cherish the earth.

They chastise me for my decision to become a vampire, as if I had another option on my deathbed. But in that same breath, they too broke a promise when they performed that spell. The witches have never been anything more than hypocrites.

"How are you feeling?" Jasik asks, breaking my concentration.

I shrug, not looking at him. I know he wants honesty, but can he handle my truth? I am scared and angry and unsure of my future. I do not know what it means to be linked to a witch, and the only person with the ability to unveil the truth has no intention of aiding me now.

I am not even sure if she is alive.

I freeze, a cold ache nestling deep into my bones.

If Mamá dies and we are linked, will I die too?

"Ava?" Malik says.

I blink away the picture being drawn in my mind to glance at him. He looks eerily similar to his younger brother, with only minor differences. Both are tall and muscular, but Malik has a much bulkier frame. Jasik is leanly muscled, making him look much younger than his older brother, even though I am sure they are only a few years apart.

"Huh? What?" I ask.

I try to see the vampires, but all I see is a vision of myself dying. But I do not die a mortal death. Instead, my heart implodes, my body combusting into a million tiny grains of ash and dust. In one single moment, everything that I am is *gone*. I leave nothing behind—no traces, no memories of the life I lived.

I am shaking, eyes lost in a haze of things that have not even happened yet, things that might *never* happen. My vision blurs, and I do not sense the vampire who comes to my side. I feel an arm wrap around me, pulling me tightly, and then I feel another. Cocooned between the two vampires, I relinquish my hold on my strength and burrow my face into an unknown chest.

Finally, I release my pain, my agony, my fear, and my doubts. I do not know how long we stand like this, but by the time I have finished, I am utterly exhausted. My eyelids are heavy, my legs weak, and I worry I cannot finish the hike to Amicia's nest. So I rely on the vampires' strength to find my way home.

Every time I find my way back here, I am amazed by the manor's beauty. The forest breaks into a small clearing, and I stumble upon the vampire nest I never knew existed in Darkhaven. Amicia and her vampires have resided here for years, all while I was patrolling these very woods.

The manor is three stories tall with breathtaking Victorian architecture. It houses startling overhangs, sharp edges, and rows of stained-glass windows. Smiling, I stare at it from the tree line.

Finally, I made it home. I escaped, and I relish in the thought that I will never experience the wrath of the witches ever again.

The moment I come face-to-face with the short fence that encloses the manor, I am awash with joy. There is something about this house that makes me feel safe. There is an aura to it. If this house could talk, it would spill endless secrets about the goings-on over the years. It has borne witness to horrific acts of violence and vengeance, but it has also offered security and warmth to souls lost after death.

The surrounding fence is formed by slabs of iron wrought together. Each point of the daggers ends in two sharp slabs of metal that form tiny crosses. My gaze trails the fence as I begin my descent into their world, into the world I was cast out of.

I reach for my metal cross, curling my palm around the peaks. The moment my skin comes into contact with the religious relic, nothing happens. I do not burn. I do not feel safer or protected by what this symbol represents. I just feel... empty. I feel nothing at all.

I sigh and release the cross. Letting my arms dangle at my sides, I take another step forward. The moment I pass the threshold, I feel at ease. I shield my eyes from the moon's bright rays and search for the weather vane. Comprised of a sharp, startling spear, it sits prominently at the forefront of the manor's highest peak.

"Everything okay?" Jasik asks.

Tearing my gaze from that which I seek, I glance at him and frown.

"What do you mean?" I ask.

"You just...seem different," Jasik says.

I try to smile, but I know it does not reach my eyes. The truth is, I *am* different. The only thing I have to hold on to right now is that I am experiencing this place all over again. As if I have never visited before, I am starstruck by the manor's beauty. I suppose after being held hostage and nearly murdered, my vision of life has changed.

I do not respond to his accusation as I walk the cobblestone path toward the manor. The overgrown grass is dead now. It crunches beneath my boots as I make my way closer to what awaits inside. The weeds that once ran rampant through the yard are dried into bushy heaps of dead brush. In the spring, when the warmth returns, they will be rejuvenated, becoming uncontrollable once again.

I allow the hand railings to guide me up the steps. Slowly, I ascend, with the vampires trailing closely behind me.

Perched on the wraparound porch is the same gargoyle I have seen for months now. Over the course of my time with the vampires, the two gargoyles I first encountered have been moved. When I first arrived, they were squatted on either side of the cobblestone walkway that leads visitors directly to the front door. Eventually, one was moved to the back door and the other was placed at the top stair.

Made of hard stone that has been tainted a dark-gray color over years of elemental exposure, the gargoyle is a hellish creature. It looks like a demon who might stand at the gates of hell, and the irony of this being protecting the vampires is not lost on me. I smile when I see him, my fingertips already tingling at the thought of touching his smooth head.

I reach for him, lightly grazing his smooth scalp. Sometimes, I wish he could come alive, but then I think, for all

I know, he does. Jasik once told me gargoyles protect vampires during times when they are weakened. These daylight saviors ensure no one invades our home when we slumber, and if that is true, then they do come alive. When bathed in sunlight, they can finally stretch their wings and soar. Only at night, when we are at our strongest, do they finally rest.

When I reach the front door, I grasp the knob. Halting, I close my eyes and listen. I place my other palm flat against the stained-glass window and wait for motion inside. I hear nothing. I feel nothing. I sense *nothing*. There is only silence and darkness and a hollow void where once lived a vibrant, powerful soul.

I sigh, twist the knob, and walk into the foyer.

The house is dark. When the vampires close the door behind me, I jump at the sound, spinning on my heels to meet a very confused Malik. Jasik is also eyeing me curiously, and I wonder how I must look to them. Suddenly hyperaware that I am basically a human in the midst of a vampire nest, a knot forms in my chest. It takes everything I have to push it down and smile at my friends.

"Ava?"

A familiar voice calls to me.

Holland.

I spin to see him. He is rushing toward me. The drink he is holding is sloshing around his mug, spilling over the sides. By the time he reaches me, it is almost gone, and the trail of dark-brown liquid left in his wake pools on the hardwood floors.

When he is close enough to see me in the streams of moonlight illuminating the manor, he drops his mug completely. It crashes to the ground, smashing into several pieces. He does not move, his gaze scanning, assessing every inch of my face.

"Oh, Ava..." Holland whispers.

He reaches for me. Ever so lightly, his fingertips graze my cheekbones, and I wince when they graze my wound. I remember the awful moment Jasik nearly died right before my eyes. The witch used air magic, molding it into a fierce dagger that penetrated his torso. When it burrowed completely through his flesh, it shot through the air, slicing my cheek in the process.

I close my eyes, remembering each harrowing second of the attack. I touch the wound with my fingers, not daring to stray too close. Still, a jolt of terror rises in my chest—but not because of what happened. Because of the startling truth, because of what this wound represents.

I did not heal.

"What did they do to you?" Holland asks. His voice is a hush, but in the silent manor, his words echo all around me, growing louder with each passing second.

Unable to face the darkness any longer, I stare into Holland's brown eyes. His skin is pale and sunken. His eyes outlined by deep divots, betraying his many sleepless nights since he arrived at the manor. He came to aid me many moons ago, and he simply never left. He spends his days researching my condition, and he spends his nights training with me. In all that time, I never wondered how—or *when*—he finds time for himself.

His hair is a floppy, tangled mess. He must catch me staring at it, because he runs a hand through his soft curls, attempting to smooth their frizzy edges. He does not succeed.

I pull him into a tight embrace, never feeling quite so emotional before. I was eager to escape the witches, and in doing so, I claimed a vampire nest as my home. The thought that this might not be the safest place for a newly mortal creature did not occur to me. But with Holland here, I remember that these vampires have no interest in hurting the living. They just want to *be*, to exist in peace. I am overrun with guilt as I hold on to Holland, squeezing him until he grunts.

By the time I release him, I realize we are not alone. Amicia is standing beside me, her crimson eyes sparkling as she stares at me. Her shiny black hair is sleek and brushed back. Her lacy gown hides her smooth dark skin. When she smiles, she bares two fangs. I stare at them as I smile back at her.

Silently, I apologize for everything I have put her through. During a time in my life when I was ousted by my very family, she took me in. And I have been nothing but a problem ever since.

"Is it...okay if I stay here?" I ask her.

She sighs. "Oh, Ava. I expect nothing else."

Her admission relieves my anxiety, but the truth of my situation is that this is only the beginning. I have a lot of explaining to do, and I have a lot of research ahead of me. I might have been lost before, but now I have no idea where to start. How do I find a book on ancient spells? How do I find information on cursing a creature I never knew existed?

"Where are the others? Hikari? Jeremiah?" Amicia asks. Her gaze diverts from me to the vampires behind me, and I cower.

"We were separated," Malik explains. "They..."

Amicia stiffens as Malik trails off. Her face pales, and her jaw clenches. I see the fear in her eyes, but in a blink, it is gone. Her worry over her vampires is replaced by something I know all too well.

Rage.

If her vampires do not return home safely, I can assume Amicia will bring her anger to the witches, and she will stop at nothing to enact her revenge.

"Tell me everything," she says.

Her voice is strained. Her words are needle sharp, and they dig their way into my muscles. I shake away the feeling, but it never truly leaves me. Amicia has always had a way about her. She is strong, defiant, and unusually patient with me. If the others do not make it back, she will ask me to make one final choice, and I will. I will avenge our fallen even if it means laying down my own life. I owe them that.

We find our way into the adjoining parlor while Malik explains the events that led us to this moment. Amicia does not speak as she silently absorbs every detail Malik recites. I sense her ever-growing fury, and I keep my gaze averted from hers.

Instead, I focus on Holland, who is paler than usual. He listens on, and each passing second, he visibly grows sicker. I remind myself that Jeremiah is his ex-boyfriend, and the two have made it clear they still harbor feelings for each other. Their breakup was over a disagreement—probably something trivial—and they never made amends. Now, he might not get the chance.

I know how that feels. That same agony washed over me when I thought Liv was taken by a rogue vampire. I blamed myself, for I did not believe she would have been in the crosshairs of a rogue vampire if not for my constant nagging. I wanted her to become a strong fire witch, regardless of the costs. I did not know she would become a pawn in my mother's twisted games.

I look away from Holland, not able to bear the truth of

his pain any longer. I have only been gone for a day, and I did not believe the manor to have changed in that short amount of time, but it has. It is as if I see everything with new eyes. I do not smell the drying pages on the first-edition books that line the walls. I do not feel the heat of the fire as it roars in the fireplace. I do not see the layer of dust coating the game of chess Malik and Jasik refuse to finish. The house feels as dank and empty as my soul.

"Ava?" Amicia says.

"Hmm," I say.

I glance at the vampires, noticing everyone is looking at me with curious gazes. Once again, I was lost in thought, too busy worrying about my own problems to care about the chaos tearing apart Amicia's nest. I hate what I have become. What happened to that selfless girl? Where did she go?

"What did you say?" I ask, embarrassed.

"Do you know anything about this spell?" Amicia asks.

I shake my head, defeated.

"Holland?" Amicia says.

He is silent for a moment. His eyes are glossy, distant as he searches the depths of his mind. I pray he will uncover some hidden meaning, some unconventional truth to what has happened to me. Maybe together we can defeat the witches for good.

Amicia clears her throat, and Holland blinks away his memories.

"No, I do not know this spell, but it sounds a lot like the black arts," Holland says.

My breath catches, and I sit in silence until my lungs burn. When I cannot take it anymore, I gasp for breath, quickly catching the attention of everyone in the room. But I do not move. I do not speak. I am focused solely on Holland's words, praying he has the knowledge to help me, for I know nothing about black magic.

"Can you reverse it?" Amicia asks.

He glances at his hands, fidgeting with his cuticles. It seems like hours—*days* even—pass before he finally looks up at me. When he does, I want him to look away. I want to smack the darkness from his eyes and replace it with the embers still burning within my soul. Mamá's spell might have extinguished my fire, but it is still there. It still flickers in the dank depths, waiting for one final burst of air to light it aflame once again.

"I am sorry, Ava, but black magic..." Holland says, shaking his head. He swallows hard, and I watch as his Adam's apple bobs in his throat.

"What are you saying?" Jasik asks. "What does this mean for her?"

Holland exhales sharply. "Black magic is almost always irreversible."

Irreversible. The word sinks into me, like a dagger to my belly. It roots itself deeply, and I know it will never wiggle free.

"How can that be?" Amicia asks.

"Magic comes from the earth, and in order to do something truly dark, there is a cost," Holland explains. "Witches cannot simply snap their fingers and make their wishes become reality. We have limits."

"And in order to bypass these limits, a witch might turn to black magic?" Malik asks.

"Yes, but there is always a cost," Holland says.

"I suppose that makes sense," Amicia says. "We do not want this magic at the hands of just anyone. Only those willing to bear the burden of casting such dark magic will dare to delve into these arts."

"Exactly, and unfortunately, once the spell is performed and the cost is paid, there is no going back," Holland says, voice dark.

"How can we be so sure *this* spell has a cost?" Jasik asks, ever hopeful.

"There is always a cost, Jasik," Holland says. "Sometimes, it is as heinous as a life for a life. Every spell is different. There is no telling what cost the witches paid to perform such a dark spell."

"But this cost, the witches must bear it?" Malik asks.

I understand his unspoken meaning. If those who perform the dark spell are the ones who bear the greatest cost, then we have nothing to fear. We did not cast black magic, so Malik assumes we should be safe. But I know better, because I know something the vampires do not know.

"Yes, the witches will bear the brunt of it," Holland says.

"That is good news, then," Malik says. "Ava should be okay."

I do not look at them. I do not admit what happened, because I cannot bear to see the truth of it flash before their eyes.

Holland's words reaffirm what I already know. I am doomed to spend the rest of my days as an empty shell, my soul blackened by the chasm my own mother forced me into.

Unfortunately, I am not alone.

Deep inside of me, Mamá is there. Her essence coats my own, blending together, reminding me that we are *linked*. Forevermore, she will always be there to guide me, to usher me to her side, and for the first time in my life, I can envision no greater hell.

FOUR

The silence in the manor is so loud, it hurts my head. I finger my temples, feeling the onset of a migraine burrowing into the depths of my skull. It has been far too long since I have experienced such mundane pain, and I am not even sure how to treat it. I can feel the vampires' gazes on me, watching silently as I sink deeper into my weakened, mortal state.

The longer I sit and assess the damage done, the worse I feel. When I can no longer mentally check my wounds, I open my eyes, and they all look away. In unison, their gazes are averted, and they all pretend to be far too interested in banal things—the dust-coated chess pieces on a nearby table, the leather-bound books on shelves, the crackling logs in the fireplace, the floorboards that creak with every uncomfortable twitch. All at once, I feel like I am an animal in a cage or a fish in a bowl, and it makes me uneasy.

I toy with the hem of my shirt, hyperaware of how desperately I need a shower. My fingernails are chipped and dirty, blood is caked to my skin, and my frizzy hair clings to my forehead. My scalp is itchy, and I am certain the stagnant odor in the room is coming from me. The vampires do not react to my stench, but I know it lingers in the air.

When the front door crashes open, I jerk upright, muscles tight. My body aches at the sudden jolt, but I land on my feet.

The pain resonating from my lower back, where I greeted the frozen earth far too many times tonight, is reaching ear-piercing volumes, but I try to ignore it. I do not want the others to witness just how injured I actually am.

As I slowly trudge to greet our visitors, wincing with each step, the other vampires are already making their way toward the foyer. Someone shuffles inside, and I struggle to see who has come in. I suck in a sharp breath when I try to stand on my tiptoes. The pain radiates down my legs, and it offers no better view. The wall of vampires, all with their backs to me, are impeding my vision, and I have just about had enough of it.

Finally, I push through and find Jeremiah, bloody and burned, leaning against the adjacent wall, and Hikari, seemingly as badly wounded but still offering support to her fallen brethren. Jeremiah attempts to stand upright, only succeeding in falling against Hikari, his towering frame comical beside her tiny stature.

I watch, unmoving, as the others rush to their sides, scrambling to usher their fallen comrades into the parlor, where they can hopefully rest. Amicia disappears down the hall, running toward the kitchen. In a flash, she is gone, my mortal eyes unable to keep up with her blurry image.

By the time Jeremiah and Hikari are seated, she has returned with an armful of blood bags. Not bothering to warm them in a mug, Amicia rips open the tiny plastic bags with her teeth before she guides the flowing crimson liquid into Jeremiah's mouth. Malik mimics Amicia's actions, feeding Hikari.

The wounded vampires slurp down heaps of blood, the noise echoing through the entire manor, and my blood runs cold. My stomach churns at the sight of the thick, juicy substance, and bile works its way into my throat. When their mouths overflow and blood seeps down their chins, splattering on their chests, I groan. Turning away, I jerk around in my seat, grunting at the flash of pain behind my eyes. I pray my face does not betray how startlingly different I truly am now.

When I finally regain my composure, I look up to find Jasik watching me. I am not sure how long he was watching me, but now, he stares intently, his face lacking emotion. Behind his blazing crimson irises, I am certain he realizes just how serious my condition is. The witches committed a hateful act, and now, I must bear the consequences. In a manor full of vampires, I am mortal. And I am hungry. My stomach growls, reminding me that I reside in a house with a kitchen stocked full of blood, not bagels.

I frown and look away, not able to maintain eye contact with my possibly *former* sire. He might not be able to show it, but I feel his pain, his longing, his disbelief. It matches my own agony. And I cannot bear witness to that truth in his eyes. I am too busy dealing with my own roller coaster of emotions.

When Jeremiah and Hikari finally stop feeding, they have drained at least a dozen blood bags. Exhaling slowly, I dare a peek. The empty bags are piled on the floor, sucked almost completely clean.

For the first time since the battle, I see the vampires clearly. The devastation of the witches has had far too great a toll on them, and I know it is my fault. We all could have died tonight. Thankfully, both are slowly healing. Their wounds, fresh and raw, are closing. But even though they no longer bleed, I know they are not out of the woods yet.

Jeremiah wipes his damp forehead dry. Outside, a raging

snowstorm is settling upon us, and I cannot help but think the roaring fire is a courtesy to Holland—and to me. I have to keep reminding myself that as a mortal, I need these luxuries I did not require just yesterday. I need food and water and warmth during these cold winter months.

I shake my head, not wanting to focus on what *I* need. I meet Hikari's gaze, and she nods at me. She wants me to believe she is okay, and though I know she will be fine, her desire to assure me of her status carves a hole in my heart. After everything I have done, after sending these vampires to the brink of death far too many times, *why* do they keep loving me?

At the sight of her, I suck in a sharp breath and hold it far too long. She must have fought a fire witch, because her clothes bear the marks. The fabric of her jacket is scorched, leaving only threads in some areas. Beneath the worst of it, even her T-shirt is gone, revealing flesh never meant to be bared. Her flesh beneath is bright pink and raw, and she grunts as muscles thread together, slowly healing the damage done. When Malik attempts to get a better look, she winces.

I grind my teeth, wondering if Liv is to blame. It would take a strong firestarter to do this much damage, but the culprit is not exactly powerful. A truly great fire witch would have summoned enough strength to kill them. Whoever did this is a novice. She is strong enough to harness fire's power, but she is too weak to kill a vampire. I hate that I have just described Liv. How has it come to this?

Jeremiah curses, catching my attention. If not worse, his wounds are just as bad as Hikari's. Both squirm under inspection, crying out when even the lightest touch ventures too close to open wounds.

Jeremiah tenses when Holland shuffles over to his side.

Nestling himself beneath his former lover, Holland places Jeremiah's head on his lap and attempts to soothe his pain. He thumbs circles on his forehead, rubbing away ashy skin with moisture from Jeremiah's hair.

I witness the exact moment Jeremiah's pain is replaced with his desire to love Holland again. I watch as the anger he was holding diminishes, and his eyes soften. The witches have brought tragedy to Darkhaven, and finding something as special as love bloom in the wake of their devastation offers me a renewed hope that I too will be okay.

But in this moment of clarity, I remember something I never should have forgotten.

"Where is Will?" I ask, instinctively searching the dark foyer with my gaze like he might emerge from the shadows in some great surprise. I know he is not there, but still, I look for him, hoping he will prove me wrong.

The room falls silent, and as I slowly return my gaze to the wounded, I fear what the vampires will say next.

"Ava..." Jeremiah says, breathless. He grunts when he shifts to sit upright, but Holland holds him down. Aiding him, Amicia rests her hand on Jeremiah's shoulder. He protests momentarily but quickly gives up.

"Where is he?" I say again, more forcefully.

"I don't know," Jeremiah says calmly.

"We were separated," Hikari adds.

Time slows, the room spinning. I search through my memory, reliving the last moment I saw Will. He willingly charged head-on into the battle, intending to aid both Jeremiah and Hikari. He risked his life to help them, and they just abandoned him the first chance they could?

"What do you mean? What happened? Where is he?" I ask, voice squeaking. I refuse to believe they would do that. They might not have been on friendly terms, but he was clearly an ally. I cannot believe they would simply leave him behind.

No one responds, further fueling my anger.

"We have to find him," I say. "He needs our help."

"No," Amicia says firmly. She does not wait for the others to respond. With one word, she silences everyone but me.

"We have to!" I shout.

She narrows her gaze, angry with my disobedience, but I do not care. After seeing what happened to Jeremiah and Hikari, I need to know that Will is safe, that he made it out and is caring for his wounds somewhere in the woods. Maybe he ventured into Darkhaven. Maybe he was not hurt as badly and he is already leaving town. Wherever he is, I need to know that he is okay, and I need him to know how grateful I am for his help.

"We do not even know if he is alive, Ava," Amicia says, and my blood runs cold. I cannot hear the truth of her words. My mind is too clouded by my desperation to save Will from a horrific death—or worse, from a life of torture at the hands of his enemies. If he did not escape, then he needs to be rescued. I have to help him. Can't they see that?

"We do not know that," I whisper.

"I will not risk sending even one more vampire to face the witches," Amicia says. "In our weakened state, they are far too great a threat."

"But—"

"Enough!" Amicia shouts. She stands upright, and in her fury, she silences me, utterly stealing the breath from my lungs. "I will not discuss this anymore. The answer is no. Will is on his own."

I look to Jasik, hoping he can see the truth in my wisdom. Yes, we are weak, but we do not need to *attack* the witches. We can maneuver in darkness, in silence. We can find him and bring him here. There does not need to be confrontation or bloodshed. We are far smarter than the witches can ever claim to be. We *can* save him. They just have to want it as badly as I do.

Jasik shakes his head. "I'm sorry, Ava, but we just can't. We would not survive."

My eyes swell, and my heart aches. My throat dries, and a knot forms in my chest, threatening to steal the very beat of my heart.

"I cannot believe you all. Will helped me when no one else would," I say pointedly. "He *saved* me when the witches attacked us in the forest. He refused to leave the battle when Jeremiah and Hikari were left behind. And you just abandon him now?"

"While I appreciate his efforts, he chose to act willingly," Amicia says. "We have no ties to him, nor he to us. I will not bind our lives to his mistakes."

"So you will just let him die?" I ask, wanting her to say it aloud. I want her to admit she is no different from the very monsters we just escaped.

"He made his choice the moment he decided to stay," Amicia says.

"You mean the moment he stayed and helped *your* vampires?" I clarify.

"Yes. He was not asked to help us, and I will not be manipulated into giving my life—or their lives. He owed us nothing. We owe him the same."

I shake my head, wanting so desperately to express my

disbelief, but words are just out of reach. Understanding I will never be able to convince them that Will is worth saving, I stand, offering one final glance at the vampires I thought I knew, and I leave the room.

Having escaped to my bedroom in the manor, I now sit with my legs bent to my chest, and I am holding my knees.

I am in the shower. I already washed away the day's events, so now I sit on the tile shower floor and watch the water swirl around the drain. I scrubbed myself clean, not stopping until the water ran clear and my skin was pink, inflamed. Now raw, I ache everywhere, and the scorching heat of waterfall lava pouring down upon me is not helping. I wanted to ease the pain and still the aches. I wanted to burn the vision of Will from my mind.

But I can't.

Every time I close my eyes, I see his face. Will stares at me, and he is as sad as I am that the vampires refuse him aid. I understand they feel no obligation to help this stranger, but after everything that has happened, we could use another ally. At the very least, Jeremiah and Hikari should feel responsible. I hate that the thought crosses my mind. I am grateful they are safe, and I would never forgive myself if we lost either one of them. But their luck should not be Will's downfall. All I have ever wanted is to do what is right, but I am beginning to realize I cannot live in this world and have morals.

I burrow my face into the crevice between my knees and close my eyes. Only after I have cried my final tears and my eyes are puffy and heavy do I finally stand, turn off the now-cold water, and dry.

When I am dressed, I stare at my reflection in the mirror. The heat from my shower has coated the glass, and the steam distorts my image. I do not know how long I stand here, staring at a girl I do not recognize, but finally, after my feet are numb, I swipe away the vision of her with my palm.

When I clear the mess and see myself clearly for the first time, I become upset. I hate the picture I see. My eyes are sunken, my frame taut. My skin is pale and yellow, and my lips are cracked and dry. My irises are a muddled brown, and everything from my hair to my bones just *hurts*. I did not even know it was possible to feel pain so deeply, as if it is rooted in my very soul. I wonder if I will ever get better or if this agony will just become part of my daily life. Eventually, I will not even remember what it was like to feel...alive.

I curl my lips back and lean against the counter. With my nose just inches away from the glass, I inspect my teeth. Before I showered, I gave them a much-needed brushing, so now, my lack of fangs is even more evident. I run my tongue where they should be, not feeling the familiar protruding points.

Angry, I shriek, screaming at the mortal in the mirror. I ball my hand into a fist and slam it against the glass. An acute bite works its way through my wrist and radiates up my arm. Sucking in a sharp breath between my teeth, I cradle my wound and curse at the girl unfamiliar to me.

From the corner of my eye, I swear my reflection is smirking, but when I glance up, meeting her gaze, the smile is gone. It is just me and an unshattered mirror, where I can spend the next fifty years of my life looking at a girl I hate.

A hard knock startles me, and I jostle through a mound of dirty towels and clothes to reach the bathroom door.

"Malik?" I say when I see the vampire standing in my room.

"Please tell me you are not going to do anything stupid," he says, crossing his arms.

His gaze drops to the arm I am holding, and I freeze. He was in my bedroom when I had my outburst, so I know he heard me. But this is not why he is here. He was already visiting me when I had my momentary breakdown.

"What do you mean?" I ask, even though I am fully aware of his intentions. I do not even wait for him to respond.

Not bothering to dry my hair, the sopping wet mane is dripping down my back, soaking my T-shirt and dripping onto my bedroom floor. I push past the vampire blocking me in and walk toward my bed. As I pull back the covers, intent on getting a good night's rest, my wrist stings. I gnaw on my lower lip, hoping Malik cannot tell how much it aches and how nervous I am about his midnight visit.

"Have you been able to access your magic since the spell?" Malik asks.

I shake my head and sit on my bed.

"Then this would be an excellent time to remind you of that," he says.

"Malik," I say and run a hand through my tangled hair. "I'm tired, and I do not have time for cryptic chats. Just tell me what is on your mind."

He arches a brow. "I thought I was being clear. Let me be more pointed. You have a history, Ava, and it is not a good one. You ignore orders, disobey authority, and have the nasty habit of getting yourself into troubling predicaments."

"Yeah, so..." I say, crossing my arms. I hiss when I twist my wrist too far.

"Are you even sure you are capable of practicing magic again?" Malik asks.

I shrug.

"To be blatant, you are by no means in the position to rescue Will on your own," he says. "I hope you realize that."

"I am also not going to let him die because my coven is full of hateful witches," I say pointedly.

Malik exhales sharply, grumbling something inaudibly under his breath. He is annoyed with my persistence and inability to conform. He is right—I do push boundaries, but only when things *should* change.

"I had a feeling you would do something drastic," Malik admits.

"So you thought you would try to talk me out of it?"

Surprisingly, Malik shakes his head and, as if it physically pains him to speak these particular words, he winces as he mumbles, "I...am considering helping."

I inhale sharply, not bothering to hide my shock or my excitement. With Malik on my side, I just might be able to save Will and *not die* in the process.

"What did you have in mind?" I ask, giddy and ready to rush to Will's side.

"I just need time," Malik says.

I narrow my eyes. "I don't think so."

"Ava—"

"Malik, Will does not have much time!" I shout.

Malik frowns. "Why do you care so much about this boy? You are asking me to risk everything to save someone I do not even know."

"I don't expect you to understand," I admit.

"Is it because he is...was a hybrid as well?" Malik asks.

I shrug and wince at his use of past tense. The wound is still too fresh in my mind and in my heart. "Yes and no. I will not deny that part of me wants to save him for selfish reasons. If I do get my powers back, I might need his guidance."

"And the other reason?" Malik asks.

I sigh. "Because he does not deserve to die, Malik. Not for this. Not for us. And certainly not at the hands of *them*."

Malik exhales slowly, and I watch his chest rise and fall with each breath he takes. The seconds tick by, and I wonder if I haven't given him enough of a reason to help me. If stealing a victory from the witches isn't enough motivation, then I don't know what else to say.

"One day. That is all I am asking," Malik says.

"For what? What will you have tomorrow that you do not have tonight?"

"A plan."

I am silent as I consider my options. Can I risk going alone? Already, I am exhausted, and Malik's right—I am far too weak to save Will without the help of at least one vampire. If I plan to *successfully* execute this mission, I will need backup. Malik might be my only option.

"Just...promise me you will not be reckless in the meantime," Malik says.

I roll my eyes at him and yank the covers over my body. I burrow beneath them, bringing them up to my chin in order to keep out the chill. I sink into my pillows and stare at the ceiling.

This time tomorrow, we will rescue Will. The thought settles into my heart, and I nearly explode from it.

"You must be smart about this, Ava. You cannot withstand a coven of witches in this state. I promise I will help you, but I have no intention of dying either. We need a plan."

I nod. Glancing at him, I say, "Okay. One day."

When Malik finally leaves, the room is enveloped by the

night, and I quickly fall asleep.

But in the darkness, I do not visit the astral plane.

And when I dream, I do not see Will.

FIVE

When I wake, the sun is still a few hours from setting. I stare at the glow through my window, basking in its rays. I have not seen a sunset in months, and I plan to relish it today. It might be a struggle, but I woke with a renewed feeling on life. I will find the beauty in this hell.

I pull back my curtains and lean against the windowsill. From this height, I see nothing but snow and forest. The trees entomb us, encasing the manor in steady streams of thick trunks. It looks suspiciously like a wall, and when I gaze for too long, it begins to close in on me.

I squeeze my eyes shut, take several deep breaths, and open them again. This time, the trees are not quite as threatening. I cannot remember the last time I felt so...weak. Everything I see looks menacing and hazardous. Sometimes, I worry my fear will get the best of me, and I will never again leave the manor. I shudder at the thought of staying indoors for life.

I glance up at the sky and sigh. Like most winter days, it is overcast, with only hints of sunlight shining through when the clouds move. I wait for the moments when the rays penetrate those fluffy puffs. I pray I return to my former self. It is unfair that I am cursed to withstand daylight during the one season the sun refuses to shine.

When I face my room again, the light pouring through the almost never open window reflects off the tiny specks of dust in the air. I scrunch my nose at the sight, waving away the pollutants with my hands. I am unsuccessful because it is *everywhere*. Suddenly, I went from superhero to victim, strong to vulnerable. Now I have to worry about mundane things like allergies.

I groan, kicking my foot at the hardwood floors. I pace in circles, hating how lonely the manor feels.

The house is eerily silent, because I am the only one awake. The vampires will not venture out of their rooms until dusk, so I have far too many hours to kill.

My room is messy, and it reminds me of my room at Mamá's house. I was forced out so quickly, I did not have time to clean up. When I returned, I noticed she kept my room exactly the same. It too was full of dust.

Piles of dirty clothes are strewn across my bedroom floor. I pick up each piece and place them in the hamper I keep in my closet. When I turn back around, the room does not seem any cleaner. I make my bed and straighten the makeup table, which has somehow become a catchall for everything unrelated to cosmetics. Since I do not wear much makeup, I had to find another use for the piece.

I sit and stare at my reflection in the mirror. When I woke, I dressed quickly, mindlessly choosing the day's garments. I opted for my signature look: jeans, black boots, and a dark top. My jacket is hanging on the hook beside my door, and when the sun finally breaks free, penetrating the room, I can see the toll these past several months have had on my attire. During my time as a vampire, I have had to fix far too many ripped clothes. What hasn't been salvageable was tossed along the way. Sadly, my favorite jacket has taken the brunt of the attacks and is looking weathered. I am not sure how many more assaults it can withstand. Maybe it is finally time we both retire.

When I have sat alone in my room long enough, I make my way into the hallway, closing my door behind me. The stairs to the main floor squeak as I descend into the sitting room. A chill works its way down my spine, and I shiver. The fire in the adjoining parlor has been reduced to embers.

I consider finding wood, a match, and some kindling, because without the heat, I am cold, but there is a part of me— no matter how small—that welcomes this feeling. Because while it might mean I am mortal, it also means I am *alive*. I survived the curse, and I escaped the witches.

Since that fateful spell, I feel almost completely devoid of emotion. I feel pain and discomfort, but I do not hear the calling of the moon. I do not taste the salty sea air. I cannot see past the sinking feeling in my gut. My fear is a noose, and my legs are weakening.

"Ava?" someone says, and I shriek, turning around so quickly, I lose my footing and grab on to the banister to keep myself from falling. My heart is racing, my mind spinning. I hate that it is so easy to sneak up on me now.

"I—I am sorry. I did not mean to frighten you," Holland says. He holds his hands before him, reaching to steady me. His eyes are tired, but they are full of emotion. I envy him so much.

I clutch my chest, struggling to slow my rapid breathing, and shake my head.

"It's—It's okay. I am sorry. I am just..."

"You are just not used to being mortal," he finishes with a soft smile. He is empathetic to my situation. He too is a mortal in the midst of vampires. It is not easy being...us.

I shrug. "I guess not. It is these moments that make me worry I may never get used to my dulled senses," I admit.

"You will, but it will take time."

I nod slowly. "Yeah, I suppose it will."

But how much time do I really have?

"How about some breakfast?" Holland asks. "I bet you are starving."

I perk up at the thought of eating. He is right. I am famished. "I could eat."

He offers a wide, toothy grin and spins on his heels, guiding me through the dining room until we reach the kitchen.

The table has been adorned with a buffet of typical breakfast offerings. A jar of orange juice sits at its center, with two empty glasses beside it. Surrounding it is a box of donuts, another box of bagels, burned toast with a saucer of butter, a plate of pancakes, and another plate with eggs, crispy bacon, and sausage links. It is absolutely a feast for two.

Salivating, I take a seat. Completely mindless, like some wicked hungry zombie, I dive in. I shovel eggs into my mouth, humming with each bite. Nothing tastes the way I remember it—and if I am being honest, everything seems pretty bland— but my stomach welcomes each forkful. In my constant worry, I did not realize just how hungry I was. I feel like I could eat for days.

Between mouthfuls, I glance up at Holland. He is eating as well, but he is not quite as enthusiastic about it as I am. I smile, trying not to show any teeth, and I am certain I only succeed in looking like a chipmunk storing food in my cheeks for winter. But I do not care. With each swallow, the pain in my gut is subsiding.

"You might want to take it easy. We are not even sure you should be eating *food*," Holland cautions.

I nearly choke on my bite. When I finally swallow it down, I stare at the smorgasbord before me. Absolutely anything here could be toxic. A vampire cannot digest human food, but blood makes me queasy. Aside from trial and error, what am I supposed to do?

"Just go slow," Holland says, answering my internal question.

I push away my plate, stomach already in knots, and take a sip of orange juice. I scrunch my nose at its tartness, but I take another sip. So far, so good.

"Did you get all of this for me?" I ask. I tongue the crevices of my teeth as I wait for him to answer.

"Sort of," he says, and he takes another hefty bite of pancakes.

"Sort of?" I ask.

"Well, I am hungry too, but I thought you might enjoy a welcome-home buffet," Holland says.

I lick my lips, tasting the remains of salt and cheddar cheese, and I wipe my mouth with the back of my hand.

"Thanks, Holland," I say sincerely.

He smiles softly and reaches for my hands. Between plates of waffles and bowls of fruit, he holds on to me. "I know it has been hard, Ava, but it will get easier. Just give it time."

I sniffle and nod, glancing over his shoulder at the world beyond the manor. The sun has broken through the clouds. Shining down, it illuminates the remnants of a winter storm. Everything is white and icy, and it all sparkles. The window is frosted in the corners, and the world looks like a postcard.

The snow looks like a soft, wintery blanket, but beneath

those depths, danger lurks. A mortal like me cannot patrol the woods the way I have been hunting. All at once, everything is dangerous. The predators that reside in the woods, the low temperatures, the hidden brush, the icy sea... Any of these things could seriously harm me. Or worse... I shake my head, trying to remove the images flashing behind my eyes.

"Are you okay, Ava?" Holland says, breaking my concentration.

I open my eyes to find him staring at me. He is frowning, his forehead creased by his concern.

I shrug and opt for honesty. "I have been better."

"Do you want to talk about what happened?"

I shake my head, hoping to keep out the encroaching memories, but they flash before me nevertheless. I have never felt so out of control before. I cannot even keep my thoughts in check.

"I think it might help you, and maybe it will help me," Holland adds.

I frown. "What do you mean? I thought you said this is unbreakable magic?"

"I—It... I mean," Holland says with a sigh. "I am not going to lie to you, Ava. You are in a pretty serious predicament, but I also will admit that I am not a scholar on the black arts."

"Do you think we can reverse their spell?" I ask, already knowing the answer.

"Not on our own," Holland admits. "If it is even possible at all..."

I lose myself in my thoughts. What is the point of reliving this nightmare if Holland is not strong enough—or smart enough—to find a way for me to break it? I feel hexed, and there is no telling how far this spell will go. Who is to say the witches are done casting their spells on me?

"I know you are scared, but I need to know what happened," Holland says.

I exhale sharply and nod before I begin.

"Mamá lured me by lying about Liv's disappearance," I say. "She was never really missing."

Holland hangs his head low, processing my words. He sits back in his seat and crosses his arms over his chest, prepared to give me his full attention, so I continue.

"But everyone already knew that," I say. "Everyone else saw her deception for what it was."

"You cannot blame yourself for caring too much. You are a good person, Ava, with a good heart. That is not a bad thing."

I shake my head. "No, but it gets me into some bad situations."

Holland does not respond. He does not need to. He cannot refute the truth. If I did not care so much, I would not have tried over and over again to help my former allies. If only I could have abandoned them the way they ousted me, my life would be so different right now. I might not even have stayed in Darkhaven.

"After I met Will..." I say, my heart burning at the sound of his name. I glance at the clock. I am still several hours away from sunset, from Malik's deadline. Silently, I pray he can hold out that long. I do not know what torture the witches are bestowing upon him, but I hope he knows I would never abandon him.

"I know you care for him," Holland says, breaking my trance.

I blink and focus on Holland once again. "I do. In a short time, he proved himself as an ally. And we could really use some of those."

Holland smiles, but it does not reach his eyes. Like the vampires, he is cautious of Will. He does not trust him yet, but in time, they all will. They will see he is a friend, and we certainly cannot have too many of those.

"The witches attacked us in the forest, but they did not seem intent on hurting me. Now, I understand they were only after Will. They were hunting, and they were probably watching me the whole time."

I remember that night so vividly. Everything was orchestrated. Mamá knew I would patrol, and she knew I would stop at nothing until I discovered the truth. They were waiting for me. I walked right into their trap.

"Can you tell me about the actual spell?" Holland asks.

I search my memory, trying to find something, *anything*, that might be helpful, but I come up blank. My defeat must be written all over my face, because Holland frowns.

"Anything at all could be useful," he adds.

"I—I do not remember much of the actual spell," I admit.

"Do you remember anything they said? What did they chant?" Holland leans forward, resting his elbows on the table and clasping his hands in front of him.

"I do not know. I am not even sure it was truly Latin. I did not understand what they were saying. Honestly, I could barely hear them. The sun was rising, and I was panicking, and all I could do was stare at Will and watch as we were about to die."

I sniffle, shaking, and rock back and forth in my seat. Gnawing on my lip, I try to slow my sputtering heart. I cannot keep reliving this moment. I must move on from it.

"What else do you remember?" Holland asks.

"I remember begging my mother to save me. I remember

the look on her face. She did not care. She did not look scared about the possibility of watching her only child being burned alive." I cannot help the hate that laces my words. I am so angry with her. Mamá's actions were unforgivable. I hope she knows that.

"I am so sorry, Ava."

Holland tries to touch me, but I jerk away.

"Do you remember what they had on the altar?" he asks, pretending he did not notice my physical lurch as he tried to touch me.

I freeze, mentally assessing every inch of the tree stump. Situated almost at the center of Mamá's backyard, I know this altar well. I grew up decorating it, learning the proper placement of relics meant to represent the elements and the strongest parts of each spell we cast.

"I do," I say.

Holland catches his breath and waits for me to continue.

"They had the typical items to represent the elements—candle for fire, sea salt for earth, feathers for air, a chalice for water, the third eye emblem for spirit—and a golden sphere to represent the sun."

Holland nods. "We assumed they harnessed the energy of the sun to complete the spell, but this does confirm it."

"Does that help to narrow down your findings?" I ask.

"I have not found much," Holland admits. "I have never encountered a coven willing to commit such an act. Using the black arts is forbidden. There is a universal law in place, which you are well aware of. The fact that they even felt the need to dabble in such dark magic shocks me."

"I guess they desperately wanted to find a way to get rid of me once and for all."

Holland shakes his head. "I do not think they ever intended to hurt you. They risked their own lives to perform a spell they had no business casting."

"But I could have died."

"I am sure they were praying it would not come to that," Holland says.

I sigh. "You do not have to defend them, Holland."

He throws his hands up in defeat. "By no means am I condoning what they did. I am just saying, I kind of understand it. That does not make it right, but who would not risk everything for family?"

"Unfortunately, I think they were more focused on eliminating an *abomination* than actually saving my soul."

"The irony here is they risked their own souls in the process," Holland says.

I frown. "What do you mean?"

"I have never encountered someone who actively explores the black arts," Holland says, "but I have heard of witches who have attempted to harness a great deal of power. This level of magic is not innate to us, so a witch would need to source it from something inherently powerful, like the sun."

"What happened to these witches?" I ask. "The ones who tried these powerful spells?"

"These are complicated, dangerous spells, Ava."

I nod. "So what happened to them?"

"They died," he says plainly.

"They...died? What do you mean they *died*?"

"Witches are mortal beings, Ava. Our bodies cannot contain that much power. Granted, the witches I have heard about attempted these spells alone. Your spell was performed by an entire coven. I suspect they did that to limit the burden on one witch. Everyone took a piece of that power, and together, they used it in unison to...alter what you were."

"This sounds *insane!*"

He smiles. "It really does, but magic is not exactly normal. The insanity is what gives us life, power."

"What is going to happen to them?"

"I am not sure," Holland says, but his eyes gloss over. I know this look well. He is searching his mind, replaying the many scenarios until he comes up with something that fits. Malik has the same look in his eyes when he covers battle plans during our training sessions.

"Holland," I say sternly.

He blinks several times, clearing his gaze. "Ava..." He shakes his head.

"Just tell me."

"If they released the energy back into the earth, then they might be okay," he says, ever hopeful that the witches finally did something right. Doesn't he know them better by now? They *never* do what is right.

"And if they did not?"

He exhales sharply. "If they choose to keep the energy, to make themselves stronger—"

"Which I can see them doing," I interrupt. *And I know you can too.*

"Well, if it is too much, they will not be able to contain it. They will die. Probably slowly."

"And if it is not enough to actually *kill* them?"

"They will go mad," he says. "Piece by piece, their psyches will collapse to a magic they were never meant to carry."

I sink back into my chair, replaying our conversation over and over again in my mind. I would like to think I have not become so heartless that I would wish death on my former coven, but they have conditioned me to hate them. Now that I might get revenge, I am not sure how I feel. I know one thing, though. I will not rush over to warn them. They brought this doom on themselves.

"Ava, are you okay?" Holland asks, bringing me back to reality.

"For so long, I risked my life to protect them. This very thing terrified me. The thought of losing those who I loved..."

"It must be difficult to accept that your mother may die soon," Holland says.

And all at once, the world stops spinning. My heart sinks deep into my stomach, where my food coma was already hardening into knots.

"What is it? Ava? What is wrong?" Holland says. He leans forward and grabs on to my hand. He grips it firmly, tightly, never loosening until I speak.

"I remember something," I admit.

"What?" Holland asks, breathless.

"For them to perform this spell, I had to be linked to something earthly," I say.

Holland frowns, processing my words.

"I was linked to my mother."

SIX

The walls of my bedroom are closing in on me. Slowly, they creep closer. The floorboards splinter and crack, giving way to a far greater force that has its sights set on me.

Even my bed frame, with its flowing waves of sheer fabric meant to symbolize an escape, looks like a prison. I try to envision the tropical paradise I once saw when I looked at this room, but I cannot see it. All at once, the world is crashing down, and it is taking me with it.

Desperately trying to calm my nerves, I run a hand against my neck, swiping away the moisture that is dripping down my back. What sweat I do not catch soaks into my T-shirt. Suddenly, I am acutely aware of how moist my clothes are. I am drenched in sweat from fear, from the mere thought of slowly descending into madness. I realize now that this will be my only awareness of it, for the insane do not know they are mad.

In these last moments of undeniable truth, I shake out my limbs and crack my neck, hoping to ease the growing tension swarming within me. Unfortunately, it does not work. Slowly, I am slipping into the unknown, and I cannot find my way out.

"Just relax," I say to the empty bedroom.

I must maintain my composure. Already lost in a channel of nihility, I cannot jump into yet another pit.

Darkness swarms all around me, threatening to overthrow what little sense I have left. I worry this is it. This is my last moment of peace.

I think this is what insanity looks like. I replay my conversation with Holland over and over again in my mind; it loops endlessly, and I cannot stop it. The moment he discovered my link to Mamá, Holland promised he would stop at nothing to sever it. He assured me I would not succumb to the witches' affliction. I believed him. But now that he is gone and I am left with nothing but my looping thoughts, I am beginning to doubt him.

I stare down at my badly shaking hands.

"You need to calm down, Ava," I say softly. "Get it together."

I remind myself I will not die from this curse, and I will not go mad either. Holland is confident, but even as I attempt to convince myself, I am not so sure. I force myself to question everything and everyone.

Is Holland smart enough? Strong enough? Does he have enough connections to outsmart the witches? I imagine it is not easy to break a black magic spell, so why is he so sure he can figure out a way to save me?

"Stop!" I shout.

I must stop second-guessing my friends. They are not deserving of such disrespect. They are not the reason I am in this mess. I did this. I made this happen.

Sitting on the edge of my bed, I think about what the witches have done. They are sociopaths and murderers, and it took such a severe betrayal for me to finally see them clearly. And when I look at them now, all I see is madness. But I know it is too soon for their behavior to be the effect of the spell. So if their normalcy looks like insanity, what is to come? What should I expect as this magic eats away at their insides, leaving only a dark, barren fissure where their hearts once beat?

I shiver when I think about falling victim to such vicious magic. This is why the black arts should never be dabbled with. Even a coven should not risk harnessing such power. It pains me to think Mamá felt as though she had no other choice than to cast such a dark spell. Does she hate me that much? She would risk not only my soul but hers as well? And what about the souls of her coven? Does she not care for anyone? Does she believe me to be such an abomination that all of Darkhaven must fall in order to be rid of me? How can I come from such a despicable woman? I hate to think it is her blood that runs through my veins.

I sigh and sink my head into my hands. My eyes swell from frustration, and my temples burn where I rub them profusely. I feel a headache coming, and I am desperate to save myself from yet another annoyance.

Ever since Mamá cast this spell, I have felt nothing but pain and fear. I want to feel strong again, to feel *alive*, to be *free*. I want to run with wolves and smell the flowers even in the dead of winter. I want to hear the moon and connect with spirit.

All I want is to envision myself as a vampire again, but when I close my eyes, I see the black hole expanding within me. The vampire I once was is gone. She is dead, a severed chain in my withering link to that other world. I miss my world of darkness and chaos. I want so desperately to be part of it again. I want to hunt with the vampires, to patrol Darkhaven and keep the humans safe from the witches. I want my life back.

I am an hour into my pity party when there is a soft knock on my bedroom door. I glance out my window. The sun has set, and night blankets the village. Immediately, I think of Malik. His deadline is up. It is time to save Will.

I jump to my feet and rush over to the door, eager to distract myself from my impending doom.

As soon as I grasp the doorknob, I hesitate. Do I tell Malik what Holland said? I shake my head at the thought. *Of course* I tell him. He needs to know. They *all* need to know what is to come. But *when* do I tell him? When do I tell Jasik?

I squeeze my eyes shut, trying to cast out the images of my former sire. I cannot think about him right now. I do not want to remember the pain in his eyes, the hurt in his voice, or the fact that he sided with Amicia over me. He had his reasons. I am sure he assumed it would keep me out of trouble, and if Malik had not agreed to help, it just might have.

I twist the handle and yank open the door.

"Malik," I whisper, voice betraying my relief. A small part of me worried he would never show.

He smiles at me, and I step aside to let him in.

"Hikari?" I say in disbelief. "What are you doing here?"

"Malik tells me you are one vampire short of a successful plan," she says.

I frown and glance at Malik. He is silent, somber. Staring at my open window, with the curtains pulled to the side, offering a full view of what lies beyond these walls, Malik looks at the forest that surrounds the manor.

Feeling suddenly self-conscious, I walk over to him and cover the window, hiding what Malik already knows as my truth.

I am different.

Blood makes me queasy. I cannot access magic. I do not burn in sunlight.

Every hour that passes unearths a new piece, and I fear what will remain of the puzzle when we are finished putting it together. Will I like what I see? Or will I spend my final days growing old as my new family remains forever young? Will they remain by my side when I take my final breath? Or will they have long since left Darkhaven, cast out of their home by the witches who betrayed me?

"So we have a successful plan?" I say, turning back toward the others. I do not contain my excitement.

"I never said it will be *successful*," Malik clarifies.

Hikari sighs. "Do you always have to be a killjoy?"

"Okay, but there *is* a plan?" I ask.

Malik's eyes darken, his face growing somber with each passing second. He crosses his arms, and his jacket strains to cover his bulging muscles. Hikari stands beside him. The two are polar opposites, complete contradictions, yet she is just as strong. Vampires are delightfully deceiving creatures, and I ache to be one again.

"You are not going to like the plan, Ava," Hikari says.

"But it will work?" I say.

"Yes—" Hikari says.

"It *should* work," Malik interrupts.

Hikari groans and mumbles something under her breath as she rolls her eyes at Malik. Her spiky hair is shiny and black, and it glistens in the darkness. Malik ignores her protests, eyes focused solely on me.

"Are you prepared for this, Ava?" Malik asks.

I gnaw on my lip but nod. I will not deny that I am scared. I am weak, barely human. What can I offer them? How can I actually be useful? I cannot do much, but I refuse to abandon Will.

"Tell me what I need to do," I say, feigning confidence.

Malik swallows, and the room falls silent.

Hikari glances up at him, nodding sharply.

"I spoke with Holland," he says. "He told me about the link."

"Oh..." I say, voice soft.

I am ashamed I did not tell him first, and honestly, I am not even sure why I did that. It is as if the witches have an invisible muzzle over my mouth. Even from afar, I keep their secrets when I do not want to.

"We are going to use your link against them," Malik says.

"How?" I ask.

"You are going to be bait," Hikari says, grinning.

"Bait?" I repeat, frowning, not liking the sound of that. Doesn't the bait usually die?

Hikari nods, beaming, utterly confident in the plan these two vampires have developed while the others slumbered, while I was having my heart-to-heart with Holland.

"Bait," Hikari confirms.

Sneaking out of a house full of vampires, all supposedly with the keen senses needed to best even the world's greatest hunters, is far too easy.

I slip out the front door without a single hitch. I almost consider pursuing a life of crime after this, because clearly, I am an excellent silent ninja. I can sneak out of just about anywhere and not get caught. Even Mamá had been clueless.

While running down the front porch steps, my foot catches on a plank, and I tumble forward. I slide down the steps with expert ease—thanks in part to the ice storm that poured down on us last night. I break my fall but land ungracefully into a mound of snow. Flopping over, I lie on my back, staring up at the two vampires towering over me.

Hikari snorts while Malik sighs and helps me up.

Embarrassed, I keep my head down while I brush off the debris. Snow has coated my body, and I am desperate to remove the evidence.

"Are you sure this plan will work?" Hikari whispers to Malik.

My gaze darts to hers, and I narrow my eyes. *One time. I fell one time. I can do this!* I scream at her with my eyes, not daring to raise my voice. With my current luck, I will be loud enough to catch the attention of everyone inside. For our plan to work, we need to go alone.

Malik ignores her and focuses on me. His skin is pale, his irises a fiery red. He looks fierce yet indifferent, tired yet alert. Malik is most definitely a walking contradiction.

"Remember, Ava, stick to the plan," he orders. "Nothing else."

I nod sharply. His plan to use me as bait loops in my mind. As he explained, it is a last-case scenario. He and Hikari are going to attempt to lure out Will themselves, and with my help and a little luck, they just might be able to navigate Mamá's house without ever encountering a witch.

"This is not about vengeance," Malik reminds me.

"I know," I say. "This is about saving Will."

"And surviving," Hikari chimes in.

"Yes, we all must survive," Malik says.

I smile, suppressing a chuckle. "That would be important... per the plan."

Before the other vampires catch us outside, we escape through the gate. We make the trek through the forest, ever conscious of the fact that we may not be the only ones hunting these woods tonight. We keep our eyes alert for motion, fearing the witches may be planning a counterstrike. The thought makes me cringe, but I know Mamá well enough to know she will not give up without a fight.

Malik and Hikari are risking everything to help me. When Amicia finds out they disobeyed her orders, there will be hell to pay. Their punishments will not be light.

I glance at them. They both lead the way while I struggle to walk in foot-deep snow, hoping they know just how much I appreciate their alliance. They might have only agreed because of my stubbornness and inability to leave an ally behind, but I am grateful nonetheless.

I jump into each imprint Malik's large boots make in the snow, and soon, my legs ache from the activity. It feels like it has been *years* since I had a good workout, even though I know that is not true. My training sessions with Malik and Holland were both physically and mentally exhausting, but it seems those benefits did not follow me into this afterlife. Now, I feel like jelly. I feel wiggly and floppy, and I ache all over.

I swipe the sweat on my forehead with the back of my hand, breathing far too loudly for someone supposed to be sneaking around. With my eyes focused on the ground, desperately trying not to fall, I do not notice the vampires coming to a sudden halt.

I walk into Malik, the top of my head smashing against his back. He does not budge, but I yelp and grab on to him to keep myself steady. Digging my fingers into the fabric of his jacket, I maintain my hold, not releasing him even when I glance around to see what has caught his attention.

"What is it?" I whisper, breathless. My chest heaves, and I squint in the darkness. Without the vampires' heightened senses, I cannot see what is worrying them.

Unfortunately, I do not have to wait for a reply.

All at once, the forest is brighter. I squeeze my eyes shut, throwing my hand up to shield myself from the fire's bright flames. When I have finally adjusted to the drastic difference, I lower my arm and bear witness to what has halted our approach.

Malik is still silent and stiff as stone before me. Hikari is standing beside him, arms flexed, hands balled into fists at her sides. I am cowering behind them, daring a peek between the wall of vampires protecting me.

And that is when I see them. There are so many. They step forward, revealing themselves and their hiding posts. They step from behind trees and up from heaps of snow. They are dressed in white, blending into the icy forest.

Abuela steps forward, and Mamá is close behind her. They walk with an elegant grace, mouths turned up and devious glints sparkling within their eyes. I wonder how long they have been waiting here. How long have they been hunting me?

"*Hola, hija*," Mamá says.

Her words twist around me, slithering their way into my soul. Just one glance from her is enough to pierce my heart and assure compliance.

I look away, shoving my face into Malik's back. His hands are dangling at his sides, and I grab on to them.

Teetering, I whisper over and over again that I am strong,

that she has no control over me, that there is no link. I say it enough times I almost convince myself these words are true.

But then she speaks again.

"*Mírame, niña,*" Mamá orders.

I am trembling, fighting the overwhelming urge to look at my mother. She has ordered me to, and it takes every ounce of strength I have to fight her desire.

The connection linking us is threading tighter around me, and I worry it will smother me, squeezing out my breath, my blood, my complete essence until nothing remains but an empty, dead shell.

"Fight it," I whisper over and over again. "You are stronger than her."

Malik begins breathing louder, so dramatically so, it calms my aching limbs. I listen to his breath, letting it match my own. Slowly, I begin to calm, but when Mamá speaks again, igniting yet another fire in my soul, I almost break. I almost look at her. I almost succumb to her will.

Slowly, Malik threads our fingers together into a makeshift chain. He radiates power, strength. Vampires are naturally alluring, and I let his scent, his natural musk, settle over me. When he begins to trace circles with his thumb against my skin, I feel more grounded than ever before. For one brief moment in time, I believe I *can* fight this curse. I believe I am strong enough to survive it.

But then Mamá speaks, and my world crumbles.

"*¡Dije mírame!*" she screams, and I shriek. Her anger erupts from within her and boils into me. I am awash with her frustration from my disobedience, and soon, everything I am is gone, leaving only what she is.

And she is evil.

I fall away from Malik, landing on the ground. I catch my fall with my hands, but my arms sink into the earth. I look at her, just as she instructed. I do not disobey her again.

Her irises are black as night. No longer the muddled brown color I remember, they are angry and hateful, and they threaten me with death.

"*Por favor, Mamá*," I shout, begging for mercy, even though I know there will be none tonight.

I worry I was wrong to save Will. If he is already dead, then I stepped into the witches' trap for nothing. Now, I have nothing to gain and everything to lose.

"We need to get out of here," Hikari whispers. Her voice is so low, I almost do not hear her.

I glance back at Malik, but he does not look at me. He does not break his gaze, remaining ever focused on the witches. With each passing second, their numbers grow. More and more unfamiliar faces surround us, strengthening Mamá's hold over me. She is far too powerful, and I fear the worst.

She has not released the magic.

She is one smart spell away from diving steadfast into this obscure prison.

And she has every intention of taking me with her.

"We are surrounded," Malik says softly, simply. He remains strong before the witches, confident in his plan. Even as I falter, he never wavers.

Hikari scans the forest, spinning on her heels. Her eyes confirm Malik's assumption. We are surrounded.

I scramble to my feet, hands frozen from the snow. When I finally stand, Mamá speaks to me.

"*Sal del camino*, Ava," she says.

I shake my head, refusing to move. I will not step away

from the vampires, because the moment I do, blasts of fire magic will incinerate the ground. Malik and Hikari will not die because of me.

"How did you know we would come to you?" Malik asks.

"*¡Cállate, demonio!*" Abuela says.

"You do not speak to us," Mamá says, seething.

"How did you know? How did you find out we would be here?" I shout, repeating Malik's question.

A sharp gust of wind radiates through the forest. It howls through the air, shaking branches as it assaults the hibernating trees. I shiver, lip trembling. I am not dressed warm enough for such a cold night. I squeeze my hands, my fingers falling numb. The air is bitter against my cheeks, and it burns my skin.

Mamá laughs. "No one had to tell us, *mija*. We are your family. We know everything about you."

"So you knew I would come back for him," I say softly.

Mamá nods. "You are too caring, Ava. You never could leave a friend behind."

I grind my teeth, balling my hands into fists. I want to slam them against those who keep getting in my way. I came to protect my family, and that is what I will do. Mamá thinks she is smarter than me; she always has. But I know her just as well as she knows me, and she has not bested me yet.

I turn to the vampires and grab on to Malik's hand. He softens under my caress.

"Malik," I say. He breaks his gaze with the witches to meet my eyes. "You need to leave."

He frowns and says exactly what I expect him to say. "I will not leave without you."

His voice sounds so sincere, and for a moment, I fear he truly will not leave me behind.

"We are outnumbered," I remind him, speaking loudly. I need the witches to hear us. They need to know the sacrifice I am making.

"We assumed you would return without being fully prepared," Abuela says. "But as you can see, we have many allies."

I do not look at her, but I envision the smile plastered on her face. Everything about my grandmother makes me cringe. I have never hated someone so much in my life. She is a disgrace to Papá's name, and for once, I am thankful he is not alive to see what has become of his family.

As I ignore my grandmother, I keep my eyes on Malik. I only break his gaze to look at Hikari. She is holding back tears. I can see them pooling in the corner of her eyes. I never knew she could tap into such emotion—especially for me.

"We cannot leave you, Ava," she whispers.

"We may not be prepared for this fight, but they are. We are surrounded," I warn.

"It does not matter," Hikari says. "You are family."

My heart sinks, the pain washing over me almost too much to bear. I hate that it has come to this. I truly hoped we could silently stalk the witches, using the night to our advantage to save a fallen comrade.

"I would never forgive myself if either of you were killed because of me," I say. "Do not be fooled. The witches are listening now, and they are waiting for your decision. Either you walk away, leaving me behind, or you face them now."

"We have fought these witches countless times now, and we are still here," Malik says.

I soften my grip on him, and his eyes lower to my hand as it slips away. Slowly, I walk backward, putting distance between the vampires and me. The pain in his eyes is like a knife to the heart, and each step I take digs that blade deeper and deeper into me. By the time I have put enough distance between us, it has cut clean through.

"Ava..." Malik whispers. He tries to reach for me, but I pull away from him. I cross my arms over my chest, both providing necessary warmth on this frigid evening and to firmly sever myself from the vampires.

"Let me do this for you," I whisper. "If this is all I can do to save you, then let me do this."

"Ava," Hikari calls, tears glistening down her cheeks. Her voice cracks, and it radiates off the chill that is settling in my bones. I want to run to them. Seeing their reactions is too real, too raw. I do not like this, but I understand what I must do.

And it is too late for me to return. Already, I am spinning on my heels, turning my back to the vampires. I take only a few steps before I stop completely and look at the witches. It is time I make myself clear once and for all.

"Let them go," I order. "Let them live, and I will come with you."

I stare at Abuela, our gazes becoming almost painful as we each wait for the other to blink first. After an agonizing amount of time, my vision blurs from the crisp air, and I see the faintest nod from her.

I watch the witches part, carving a hole in the circle to release the vampires. Time is of the essence, for I know the witches will not be kind for long. If the vampires want to make it home tonight, they need to leave. *Now*.

"Go," I order, nodding at the opening with my head. My teeth clank from the bleak breeze working its way through the forest, and I sniffle, nose running.

Hikari takes a step forward, but Malik does not move.

"Leave. Now," I say more firmly. I am beginning to shiver so obnoxiously, it is affecting my speech. My words sound rattled and jarring, and I am losing my authoritative tone.

I clear my throat, ready to scream at the vampires to just leave already. Unfortunately, I can fake strength with my voice, but not my eyes. I know Malik can sense my fear, my pain, but if sacrificing myself means saving them, I will leap into that fire over and over again. I have always been self-sacrificing for those I love. I know how to be nothing else.

Hikari loops her arm through Malik's and attempts to drag him away, but he remains rooted. Only after I beg him, pleading with my eyes to save himself and Hikari, does he shuffle forward.

Together, the vampires leave, putting greater distance between us than the space between the witches and me. Without their strength to lean on, I feel even weaker. The vampires granted me protection, and I yearn for that safety now.

I do not move until the vampires disappear into the distance. But before the trees engulf them in darkness, I catch one last farewell glance from Hikari.

And then they are gone, swallowed by the night.

"*Mírame*," Mamá says.

I close my eyes as I turn to face her, exhaling slowly. When I open them, she has closed the space between us. She reaches for me, pulling me into a tight embrace. I stiffen at the contact. When she wraps her arms around me, squeezing me firmly, I feel ill. My insides churn, my heart stops, and my lungs clench tightly.

"I knew you would come home," Mamá says softly against

my hair. Her breath makes the loose, frizzy strands flutter.

Bile rises in my chest, and I push it down. The thought of the vampires retreating and Mamá taking me to her home makes me sick, but I cannot show weakness. I need her to believe she has won.

After all, this was all part of the plan.

SEVEN

The forest is dark, the night silent. The witches welcome me back with open arms, as if I returned to them willingly. They act as though all is forgiven, but how can I ignore my flesh being ripped apart by those I literally died to protect?

I barely remember the girl I used to be—the one who pleaded with a vampire to save her soul because she was terrified of witnessing the destruction of her coven. I never imagined my world would fall apart at the hands of those same witches.

I worry the gaping wound in my chest, where the vampire once resided, will never close. The void, the midnight abyss in my heart that I yearn to fill, is a constant reminder of what I have lost. And I lost everything at the hands of my mother. She was supposed to protect me, to shield me from the evil in this world. Instead, she broke the laws of nature. The spell she cast is eating away at her insides, and I wonder if I should warn her. We are linked now, forever bonded and eternally inseparable. Her fate is my doom as well.

I glance at her, and she smiles at me. She shows no signs, but I know that energy is there, inside of her, stealing her sanity bit by bit. I imagine she does not have much left to give.

"Come, *mija*," Mamá says. "Let's go home."

Her words wash over me, ensuring compliance. The link

formed between us controls me. An invisible force, it twines around my independence like a spring, tightening firmly and smothering any chance I have at freedom. I do not even bother fighting it anymore.

With my head down, I trudge forward, my legs heavy, navigating heaping mounds of snow blanketing our small village. I sink into its depths, desperate to escape my life—the very one I was frightened to lose many moons ago.

I am in captivity...yet again. I have to remind myself that this is different. Malik knew we needed more time, but I knew Will had none to give. This was our compromise. Imprisonment.

The witches are talking to each other, everyone ignoring me—alarmingly so. Am I not their prisoner? I imagine running away, escaping and hiding behind a tree. They are all so focused on celebrating their *supposed* win, they are not even watching me. I glance at the women who dared challenge the vampires. They are all so...confident. I envy them. There once was a time I would face even the most formidable opponents. Now, I can barely navigate the woods at night without losing my breath.

The witches are not watching me, but I feel eyes on my back. When I glance over my shoulder, I see nothing but darkness. I squint, noticing only the dark shadow of a distant silhouette. Maybe Malik is there, watching, protecting. Or maybe it is just my imagination. The witches are not the only ones who can play cruel tricks.

I hear his voice in my mind, reminding me to remain calm, to stay compliant. We have a plan. Everything will work out, and I will be okay. This time tomorrow, I will be home again. I hope.

When I look at the sky, snow swirls in circles in the air. It overtakes my vision, making it almost impossible to see those who surround me. I pretend I am alone. I am walking through the woods, patrolling the town. I am strong and safe.

The flakes seem endless as they flutter about. I hate the cold, but the snow is beautiful. It clings to the trees, wrapping the bare branches. The moon makes it sparkle and glisten, and for a moment, the darkness is pretty, the unknown is welcome. But the serenity washing over me is brief, and reality sinks in like a dagger to the gut.

When we emerge from the woods, Mamá's house looms overhead. Papá built this home decades ago, and since his death, it has fallen into disarray. The cedar planks he painstakingly used to form our shelter have turned dark gray from years of elemental abuse. They bear the truth of the many battles fought on this land. Parts are charred from fireball lashings, and Mamá simply never cared enough to cover them.

In the woods, I felt free. I could close my eyes and envision a different life. But the moment I crossed the tree line, the truth of my situation revealed itself. The air here is stagnant, with life frozen in time since Papá's demise. I stare at my childhood home, hoping blissful memories of days past will flash before my eyes. Isn't that what is supposed to happen when one's life is over? I wish for happy memories, but they never come.

The picket fence that separates the house from the forest welcomes me home. I pass through the threshold, the noose around my core tightening with each step I take. The greater the distance between the vampires and me, the harder it is to ignore my link with Mamá.

Slowly, I am sinking into a black, tarry pit. My feet are stuck, suctioned to the goo, and it hurts so much, I actually look down. Staring at my heavy legs, I see nothing but a frozen tundra, a whitewashed land.

I want to tell myself that there is no pit, no tar, no dark depths eager to swallow me whole. It is all in my mind. But I know that would be a lie, for there is no greater deceiver than the witches.

The sliding doors that lead to the kitchen are only a few feet away now, and though I walk entranced, like a sated zombie, I can feel my fear rising in my chest. I want to scream. I want to run. But I do not. I just sink further, allowing the gunk to coat my legs from foot to knee.

The moment I reach the doors, I hesitate. It is brief but enough for the witches to notice. A silence befalls the group, and I stop, waiting for their inevitable reaction.

Everything I have done today has been in preparation for this exact moment—*the return*. But I am terrified that walking through these doors means eternal confinement. What if I cannot escape again? What if our plan fails? What will become of me if Mamá refuses to release me?

Mamá places her hand on my shoulder. I do not have to glance back to see it is her. The immediate warmth that washes over me is all I need to confirm her identity. Even her touch guarantees compliance. If I am to survive this night, I must pull strength from the very depths of my soul. But now, after all that has happened, am I truly that strong? Can I withstand her torment and the link?

I glance at her reflection in the mirror, and I gasp at the sight. I imagine she is smiling at me, but I do not see joy at all. Her face, darkened by the night, has morphed into a hideous creature. Her skin is taut, her eyes sunken, and her teeth large and bright; she looks more like a skeleton—like death incarnate—than a loving mother.

I squeeze my eyes shut, suck in a sharp breath, and step into the house. I'm so desperate to put space between Mamá and me, I am willing to walk into my prison to escape her.

I open my eyes, cross my arms, and hold on to myself as I enter. I try to draw from my inner strength, pretending the palms of my hands are somehow capable of becoming energy portals. I envision this magic seeping through my hands, strengthening every inch of my frame. I stand taller, more defiant.

When the sliding doors slam closed behind me, a burst of cold air sends shivers down my spine. I chew on my lip, peering into the living room. Unfortunately, we are alone. Will is nowhere to be found.

"*¿Tienes hambre?*" Mamá asks.

"No," I say. The thought of eating right now makes my stomach churn.

"*Siéntate,*" Mamá says, and it takes all I have to fight her order. My body wants to obey, but my mind is screaming at me to stop.

"I am tired," I say, glancing at the chair Mamá is pointing to. She wants me to sit, to talk, but I cannot. Any information she gains might uncover weakness. I worry about my safety, but I also fear for the vampires. The witches used black magic against me—one of their own. There is no telling what they will do to the vampires. I simply cannot risk it.

"Come," Mamá says. "I will walk you to your room."

I shake my head, immediately chastising myself for being far too eager to escape her. Mamá narrows her eyes, and already I can tell her mind is spinning. She is frustrated with my disobedience—something her spell surely should have corrected. If she asks me about my intentions for so easily returning home with her, will I divulge our plan? I must keep the vampires a secret. My survival—and Will's—depends on it.

"You have company," I remind her. I glance at the many unfamiliar witches who have assisted Mamá in ruining my life, and I burn their faces into my memory. I hate them—*all* of them, even the ones I *do* recognize.

Mamá frowns, but ultimately, she agrees to let me go alone. I knew she would. She may be a monster, but she is still my mother. She is not the only one who can con a fool.

Before she can object and force me to stay, I turn, rushing from the room. Without being too obvious, I quickly walk down the hall and up the stairs, nearly twisting my knee when I take the top landing too quick. I stumble into my old bedroom and slam the door closed behind me. With the wood barrier between us, I can finally breathe again.

Turning, I face my empty room, sliding down the door until I plop onto the floor. I sit with my back to the barrier, knees hiked up to my chest. Closing my eyes, I listen intently to the muffled conversations downstairs, rocking back and forth until the sounds of this old, creaking house finally fall silent.

When I wake, I am lying on my side. I open my eyes and stare at the layer of dust coating the floor. I sigh, blowing a cloudy puff into the air.

I sit upright, groaning as I stretch my neck. My muscles are tight, my back stiff. Glancing around my bedroom, I take a minute to fully wake. Everything looks exactly the same—eerily so—as it did before. Just sitting in this room makes me feel uneasy, like time has stood still since that fateful day. It pains me to know Mamá has been waiting for my return, especially considering how much she has tortured me over the past several months.

When I stand, my knees crack, my joints aching. Blood rushes to my head as I rise too quickly, and I lean against the door, teetering as I maintain my balance on just one leg. The other is tingling. I groan silently as the tiny pinpricks betray a sleepy limb.

Impatient, I move away from the door before my leg has fully recovered. I limp as I tiptoe through the room and peer out my bedroom window. The sky is dark, but I do not know how much time has passed. Without the ability to sense the sunrise, I have no way of knowing the hour by just glancing at the moon.

I return to the door, and placing my ear against the wood, I listen. But I hear nothing. The house is silent, the visitors gone. I imagine Mamá is sleeping in her bedroom down the hall. With the house blanketed in darkness, now is my chance to find Will.

Slowly, I twist the knob and open my door. I peer into the hallway, which is just as dark as the night sky. I take one cautious step outside my room and glance down the hall toward Mamá's room. Her bedroom door is closed.

I move slowly and deliberately toward her room, but by the time I finally reach the end of the hall and place my hand on her doorknob, I am shaking so violently, I cannot grasp the knob.

My palms are slick, my mouth dry. I wipe my hands on my jeans and shake out my arms. Silently, I tell myself to be strong, but internally, I am still far too weak to open her door.

I back away slowly, tiptoeing until I am back at the top

of the stairs. Each time the hardwood floors creak under my weight, I freeze, choking on my breath, only daring a peek after several seconds have passed.

My heart is rapid firing in my chest, making it painfully difficult to concentrate on the task at hand. Every inhalation sounds like it echoes through the house, and I fear the sound of my breathing will penetrate the walls and doors. Mamá will be furious if she finds me sneaking around, and there is no telling what her anger will force her to do.

I descend the steps so slowly, so silently, I nearly screech when the antique grandfather clock chimes. I bite my lip so hard, I draw blood, and I fumble down a step, catching my fall before I can make too much noise. I curse under my breath, mouthing my pain as I grab on to my ankle, hoping silently in a pathetic attempt to remain quiet.

In my desperation to escape the floor where Mamá slumbers, I twisted my foot awkwardly, and now my ankle throbs with each step I take. I try to put weight on it, but it protests, a stabbing pain shooting so violently through my leg, I limp the rest of the way down the steps.

By the time I reach the bottom stair, I am breathless from trying to be quiet. It is hard to breathe, to think, to even see clearly. My mind is a rush of thoughts, my heart racing from too many emotions, my body sore. I have to believe Malik's plan will work, but I am not sure he accurately anticipated just how weak I have become.

I stare at the front door. It is only a few feet away. I could run. That would mean leaving Will behind but saving myself. The realist in me reminds me I have yet to see him. I should fear the worst, but I will never know if he is gone unless I search the entire house. If it were me trapped in this house, I would hope for rescue. That would be all I'd have to hang on to, so I cannot leave without him.

I peer up the dark staircase, hopeful I have not woken Mamá. There is no light, no sound, just an emptiness that leads to our bedrooms and altar room. I did not bother checking them. Mamá would never trust Will enough to give him his own room to stay in.

I take one long, slow inhalation to strengthen myself, and I tear my gaze away from upstairs, intent on searching the rest of the house as speedily as I can.

Already, my ankle is feeling better, so I am confident I did not truly injure it. But this experience served its purpose. It reminded me I am not invincible anymore. I need to be careful if I plan to survive.

The main level consists of the kitchen and living areas, with no real place to hide a prisoner. I do not expect human visitors, but the house has windows. If Mamá is going to keep Will captive and protect her secrets from prying eyes, she would have to keep him safe, secure. That does not leave many options.

I limp down the hall, walking past the living room and toward the kitchen. Quietly, I open the hall closet, wincing as the door creaks a little too loudly. I freeze, waiting for signs that I have woken Mamá, but the floorboards never squeak.

With shaking hands, I walk into the closet, fumbling for the light switch as I close the door behind me. I am engulfed in darkness, using my fingers to feel the rough edges of the walls.

By the time I feel the familiar bulge of the switch, I worry I have spent too much time in here. That is the beauty of the night. It never feels like it lasts as long as the day. One minute in complete darkness can feel like an eternity. So by the time I find the switch, I am certain it is almost daylight.

I must find Will quickly.

I turn on the light, shielding my eyes as it stings. I squeeze my lids closed tightly, and water pools behind my lids. It takes several seconds for me to adjust to the brightness, and with each passing moment, my anxiety triples.

When I can finally open my eyes, I sift through the dozens of hanging clothes, pushing them to the sides to carve out a small pathway to what lies beyond.

Behind the rows of dusty jackets never worn and bought only for this purpose, there is a door. I open it, the hinges freshly greased to create a silent entrance. My heart sinks in my chest, because I know what this must mean. At some point, Will was most definitely kept down here, and Mamá must have visited him. I pray he is okay.

The depths below are dark, dank. As soon as I step forward, the musty air wafts toward me. I scrunch my nose and slowly descend the stone steps. To steady myself, I keep my hand on the rail, lightly grazing the wood until I reach the bottom step.

When I reach for the cord to turn on the light, my arms are shaking. Before I yank it toward me to turn on the light, I offer a silent prayer, begging to find Will alive, safe. Because if he is not here, I fear I will never find him.

I stare into the darkness, listening intently. The light from the closet above only brightens the room to the bottom step. From there, the room is pitch black. No one even knows this room exists. Papá said it was to keep us safe. He said we could hide here if there were ever an attack we could not fight. But after his death, Mamá changed it. She turned it into something dark, something heinous. It is no longer for us. It is for *them*.

I turn on the light, illuminating the small space. I suck in a sharp breath as I take in the scene before me. Will is across the room, curled into a ball on the floor. His clothes are dirty and bloodstained. His skin is pale and taut. His eyes are swollen, his lips trembling. Lying on the dirt floor, he shivers. His breath escapes in ragged puffs, and bursts of air create clouds of dust. He breathes it in and coughs, chest heaving as he tries to catch his breath.

I rush to his side, ignoring the dulling pain in my ankle, and I fall to my knees. I position myself beneath him, resting his head on my lap. I brush his hair from his eyes, and my fingers are caught in tangles.

I whisper his name so many times, I lose count. I do not know how long I sit here, and I do not know if he is even aware of my presence, but I promise him, over and over again, that I will never leave him again. I explain the plan, whispering words of hope, but he never wakes.

Enough time passes for the sun to rise. I know this even though I do not see it, do not sense it. I never returned to my room last night, and I hear the panicked footsteps of Mamá searching for me. Eventually, she will find me down here, and maybe when she sees me with Will, she will understand why I came so willingly. But I do not care.

I hear shouting coming from upstairs, but the words are too muffled. I assume she calls for me, but I ignore her.

"Ava?" Will whispers.

His eyes flutter open, and I smile down at him. I nearly scream with delight that he has found the strength to wake. I remain calm, staying silent, fearing Mamá will rush down if she hears us.

"Will…" I say softly. I brush the dirt from his cheek with my thumb.

I have sat cross-legged almost the entire night, and my legs protest. My muscles burn from lack of movement, but I do not dare move now. Will is using my lap as a pillow, and his condition seems to worsen with each passing hour. I wonder if Mamá has even fed him since she tossed him down here. How can she be so cruel? To refuse him light, food, water, a bath.

"You came back?" he asks in disbelief.

I nod, eyes welling. "I never should have left."

He frowns and turns away from me. Grunting loudly, he manages to push himself up, refusing aid when I offer it. He scoots back until he is flush against the stone wall. Exhausted and struggling to breathe, he finally looks at me.

"You should not have come back," he admits.

"They should not have left without you," I say.

I am still upset with the vampires' decision to leave him, but I understand why they did. Malik was worried about Jasik, Hikari about Jeremiah. We were wounded and outnumbered. I cannot stay angry with them, but I can hate their decisions.

Will coughs loudly, and the floor directly above us creaks. I hold my breath, waiting for Mamá to rush down the stairs. Only when an unbearable amount of time passes do I release the breath. She never comes.

"They will find you down here," Will says.

"I know," I say, still staring at the ceiling. I pull my knees to my chest, holding them tightly.

"You should have left when you had the chance."

I sigh and glance at him. "Did you really think I would not come back for you? The only reason you are here is because of me."

"I am here because I chose to help you," Will says.

I roll my eyes, mumbling under my breath. There is no point in arguing. He and I will never agree on this.

I scan the room, searching for something that could be useful. If I can find a weapon or even some secret door to the backyard, we would not have to wait for the vampires. We could escape *now*.

But Mamá knew what she was doing when she tossed Will down those steps as if he were merely garbage. The room is barren, with only a wood chair in the far corner. I consider how I can use that to my advantage, but my ideas fall flat. The walls are stone, the floor compact dirt, and the only light dangles in the far corner by the stairs. It barely illuminates the space. This room was absolutely built to be a torture chamber. I cannot believe I once saw it as a safe place to hide.

"Ava, look at me," Will says.

I meet his gaze, giving up on a silent retreat from the basement.

"You did not do this to me."

I do not speak, but I smile softly. I know Will believes his words. I can see it in his eyes, but I will never see the world through his mind. He can spend the next thousand years trying to convince me, but he will fail day after day. And unfortunately, we no longer have years to spare.

"I need you to believe that," he says. "We make our own decisions. I wanted to help, and I knew what I was getting into. This *is not* your fault."

This is not *your fault.*

I swell with emotion. I might not believe him, but that does not make me appreciate his words any less. I did not realize how badly I needed to hear that. I do feel responsible, but I appreciate Will's attempt to release that burden, to relinquish me from my own inner guilt.

"I promise, we are going to get out of here," I say. "We are going to escape, and we are going to get our powers back."

Will frowns, tearing his gaze from mine. He swallows hard and stares into the distance. His gaze is cloudy, his mind seemingly lost in what I hope is a memory from a better life.

"What is it?" I ask, and he blinks several times, clearing his eyes.

"They used black magic, Ava," Will says. "That spell is binding. There is no *going back* for us."

"My friends are working on it," I say. "They promise they will find a way around this. They just need time."

I speak so quickly, my words spill from my mouth. I am not even sure he can understand me, but I need him to trust me, to believe me. I am terrified of the thought of Will giving up. We have come too far to give up now.

Will shakes his head. "There is no use. Do not waste your time trying."

I smack him on the leg, hard, and he winces. If I were not so annoyed, I would feel bad about hitting him so hard. But I need him to see that *this* is what Mamá does. She takes every bit of sanity you have and squashes it. She brainwashes you into believing only what she wants.

"Stop!" I hiss. "Do not talk like that."

Will looks at me, his eyes emotionless.

"Is this really a bad life to live?"

I gawk, utterly dumbfounded he would ask that.

"Are you serious right now? You are literally locked up in a dungeon. You have been here for *days*, Will. Have you even eaten? Showered? Seen sunlight? How are you even going to the bathroom? Does this really sound like the *good life*?" I use air quotes to emphasize my point.

"I do not mean *this*," he says, flailing his arms before him like he is showcasing the room. "I mean being *human*. At least we are *normal* again. Things could be worse."

"Yeah, you *could* be locked up in a basement with no way out, spending your days either starving or being relentlessly tortured by captors who are slowly going mad. Oh, wait..."

I want to shake the insanity out of Will, but I know he is too frail for such viciousness. I need to convince him to remain hopeful, but I am lost for words. How can I ask him to envision a better life when all he sees is this hell? For once, the severity of our situation is settling on me, and it makes my soul hurt.

Just as I am about to explain Malik's plan, the door to the basement opens, and a bright light shines down the steps.

I do not breathe.

I do not move.

I still myself, waiting, watching as the shadow of a figure works its way down the stairs.

I swallow the knot in my throat.

"*Hola, Mamá.*"

EIGHT

As I stare into my mother's eyes, her features seem even more somber than usual. Her discomfort washes over me, pinning me in place. Without even speaking, I know she is upset with me. I can see it in her eyes, feel it in the way she carries herself as she approaches me.

Mamá is a dark shadow starkly lit against my iridescent soul. My aura is alive with vibrant, swirling colors, but as soon as Mamá is near me, I am tainted by obsidian.

Our link grants her control no one should have over another being, and I hate it. More so, I hate that she is allowing this to happen to me, her own daughter. I should not be here. She should not have cast that spell. And we should not be rushing steadfast toward madness, ensuring our self-inflicted demise.

I can tell Mamá's clutch over my freedom is strengthening. No longer do I simply *feel* her embrace. I can *see* it now too. It is inky and black, gooey at its center and feathering out at all edges. It continues to grow, spreading so far, it has almost completely wrapped around my entire body. Every moment I spend with her, she becomes stronger, and soon, I will be completely enveloped by her presence. Mamá will cocoon me in her embrace, and she will never let go.

A year ago, I could not have imagined I would be in this

position, because back then, I never knew Mamá liked to play such cruel and wicked games. She was a sweeter, calmer woman. I rarely witnessed the anger I have become accustomed to now. I do not know what happened to her to make her such a vindictive, malicious person. Was it my transition? I try to remember a time after I became a hybrid when she was not so terrifying or hateful, but I cannot.

This is the woman who raised me. This is the person she is. She is bitter and resentful and outraged by the world. Her sullen attitude and irate nature are going to get her killed.

It does not matter why. All that matters is that she enjoys these games we play, but when the sun sets, the tables will turn. The rules will change, and I will be holding all the pieces.

Right now, when put together, I do not like the picture of my life these puzzle pieces create. It is jarring and reckless; everything is in such disarray. But with Holland's help, I can regain control. I promise myself I will sever this link no matter what it takes.

Finally, Mamá stops her slow advance when she is only a few feet away from me. I am still slouched on the ground, knees to my chest, sitting directly beside Will, who refuses to look up. But I do.

I look directly at her eyes and sit upright, keeping my head up, my shoulders straight, my back strong. I want her to know I am not scared of her or this prison. I feign confidence because I know my strength worries her. She considered me an abomination, because as a hybrid, I experienced true power. And I will get it back.

I never wanted to be a vampire, but now I cannot imagine my life without fangs or blood lust. I am engulfed in sunlight, yet I search for the shadows, always aware that I seek what I can no longer have. I am no longer a vampire, but I am not exactly a witch either. My situation is so similar to my transition as a hybrid, yet it is so different. I have never felt so alone.

My heart races in my chest, and for once, I am relieved to know Will does not have the heightened senses needed to hear it. I do not want him to worry about me or to fear for his life. We only have to survive until sundown. In the meantime, I can handle Mamá's wrath, but in his state, he cannot.

Mamá glances at Will and narrows her eyes. Her hatred for him, even though he is no longer a hybrid, is undeniable. It screams from her, penetrating the room in waves of contempt.

When her anger slaps me in the face, I feel it so deeply within my own soul, I am unsure if this hate stems from her or me. Mamá manipulates my emotions so easily, without even trying, and I fear what she will do when she realizes the power she holds over me.

I am so busy looking at Mamá, I do not see our other visitor enter the basement until she has already set her sights on me. The stairs squeak, announcing her presence, and I tear my gaze from my mother.

Abuela rounds the stairs, and with her gaze glued to mine, she strides toward me. Everything about her appearance is unsettling. Her gray hair is pulled back into a perfect bun, and her clothes are fresh and ironed. Her skin is wrinkled, her eyes dark, but she looks well rested. Nothing about her shows signs of unease. It is as if she has not tapped into the black arts as a form of discipline. From the way she carries herself, she is not even slightly worried about the repercussions of her actions.

When Abuela reaches Mamá's side, she glances at Will.

"¿Sigues vivo?" my grandmother asks. Her voice is emotionless, but a slight smile creases her cheeks. She is pleased he has survived the evening, and I fear her plans for him today.

Endless streams of magical torture loop in my mind. Visions of it dance before my eyes, and I suck in a sharp breath. It is loud enough for both captors to look at me and smile. They are pleased with my fear, and they have every intention of using it to control me.

Will does not answer Abuela, nor does he look up. He remains slouched beside me, staring at the ground. Never cemented or covered with wood planks, the floors consist of dirt, now compacted over the years of providing a safe haven when violence erupted outside these walls and I was too young to aid my allies, and it does not keep out the chill. A shudder works its way through my body, and I wrap my arms around my chest to keep myself from shivering. Everything about this house feels *cold*—from the people to the lifeless furnishings. Mamá's house does not scream *welcome*. It says *keep out. Stay away. Go home.* If only I could.

"I see you have found your friend," Abuela says. I know she only speaks English as a courtesy to Will. She wants him to hear, and understand, every word she speaks.

I nod, deciding to remain silent because I fear angering her so early in the day. Thankfully, it is the winter season, which sees the shortest days, but I still have hours before nightfall, before the vampires enact the rest of Malik's plan.

"Are you surprised he is still alive?" my grandmother asks.

I shake my head and mumble.

"Speak loudly, child," Abuela says.

A quick burst of air rushes toward me, forcing up my chin. I gasp at its ferocity, shaken my mother would call upon her magic so quickly. She uses it against me with complete apathy, interested in only dominating me.

As one of the only remaining spirit users in this coven, Mamá handles the elements with experienced ease, and she wants me to know she will use them against me if I do not show respect and obey orders.

"I said," I begin, grinding my teeth as I speak, "I am not surprised he is alive. He is a *witch*." I know this will upset her, but I can no longer bite my tongue.

Abuela narrows her eyes, brow creasing. She is annoyed I would point out the obvious, but at the same time, I am certain she expected my reaction. Witches do not harm other witches. They live by an unwritten code to maintain the peace. This is also why Mamá has found so many eager witches willing to help her hunt her own daughter.

While I am surprised they are agreeing to hunt *me*, I am not shocked by their treatment of Will. I know they do not see him as a witch, as one of *them*, even though their spell has ensured this. He may be severed from his vampire half, but he is still a hybrid in their eyes. He can do nothing to change their minds or to redeem earlier actions. He will forever be the enemy, regardless if he deserves such status.

I imagine that is why he has been treated so poorly. Not only do they hate him for what he is, but they also are using him to test my limits. What happens when they use magic against a former hybrid? How much can Will and I withstand before we break? They will find their answers by harming him, not me. Not until I deserve punishment. Unfortunately, Will cannot handle any more of their *tests*.

"What was your plan when you found him?" Abuela asks. "Were you planning to escape?"

I do not look at them, and I do not respond. They do not

need me to admit my intention. They know I will escape the moment I am given the opportunity to do so, regardless of any plan set by Malik. I am supposed to wait for him, for them, but if I find another door, I will walk through it in order to save us.

I wonder if Mamá planned for this encounter. Why else would she have not spelled me to my room like she has done so many other times I have upset her? She could have easily prevented an escape, but she did not even try to keep me in line. Already, I have failed a test.

Now, she is certain where my loyalties lie—and they are not with her, this coven, or these unfamiliar witches. I am loyal to the vampires, to those who *deserve* my trust and respect. They are my family now, not Mamá or Abuela or anyone else.

"¡*Respóndeme!*" Abuela shouts, and I wince at her scream as if her words could actually lash me. Her voice echoes in this small space, bouncing off the stone walls, amplifying her presence as I cower on the ground, fearing I will see the worst of her.

"No!" I yell, knowing she will not believe my answer. It does not matter what I say or what I do. My grandmother will make an example of this moment.

"*Mentirosa,*" Abuela says.

I shake my head and whisper, "I am not lying."

Again, I lie. I lie to save myself from her torture, even though I know that to be a worthless cause. My grandmother has planned every moment of this day. She returned from her trip to find her coven in shambles. Mamá was supposed to protect us in my grandmother's absence; she was supposed to take care of my unfortunate situation, because I was a blemish on our picture-perfect family. But she failed.

Now Abuela is cleaning up my mother's mess, and she

is making a spectacle of it. Choosing Liv as her sacrifice was all part of their plan. They knew I could not refuse to help my former best friend. I played right into her plan, and now she is playing into mine. We both fancy ourselves the cats in this game, but eventually, someone must be the mouse. I refuse to be the weaker person.

"You know what you must do," Abuela says.

Although she looks at me, I know my grandmother is speaking to Mamá. Now I see my family for what they are, and like the rest, she is a coward. She will force my mother to torture me as retribution for a crime I never actually committed. I might have fancied the idea of escaping, but that was not part of the plan.

I do not bother trying to convince her that my intentions were only to find Will, to make sure he was okay, because even though these words are true, she will never believe them.

Mamá stares at me, and I meet her gaze. I want her to look me in the eye as she strikes me down. Mamá has only struck me in anger once and it was with deep regret. I wonder how she will live with herself as she commits untold violence against me, her daughter, a *witch*, because of the order from her elder. I hope her guilt eats her alive.

A quick flash of guilt pierces her eyes, and I think she is going to cry. But almost as soon as these emotions overwhelm her, they are gone. She no longer stares at me like a mother stares at her wounded child. Instead, she looks at me with regret. But fake sympathy does not deceive me. She is not regretful of what is to come but of what *I am*.

She firmly believes my decisions have brought me to this moment, and that I deserve every slice of misery cast my way. She might be right. Maybe I do. I did choose to become a vampire, but I did it for all the wrong reasons. I did it to protect *them*, when I should have been focused on protecting *me*. Because there is nothing worse than being a witch and sacrificing yourself for those who would burn you at the stake.

I feel the sudden rush of elements erupt within the room. At first, I welcome the heat. It stifles the bitter cold, but too quickly, a sheen of sweat coats my skin. I swipe at my forehead. The humidity is making it hard to breathe, and the lack of oxygen is making me sleepy. My eyelids are heavy, my limbs weak.

I rest against the stone wall, lolling my head back to look at Mamá. Her eyes are emotionless pits, and the reality of that smacks me in the face. She does not care that she is using her magic to torture me. She just wants me to fall in line, to submit to her will. But I refuse.

My T-shirt is soaked through, and the heat is becoming almost unbearable. I ache to remove my jacket, but I will not. I do not want them to know just how seriously their elemental control is affecting me.

I try taking long, deep breaths, but the air is stifling. I think my tenacity angers Mamá, because she frowns and snaps her fingers. Almost immediately, the heat dissipates, and it is replaced by a burst of icy air. My breath releases as puffy steam before my eyes, clouding my vision as I try to maintain my tormentor's gaze.

Lip quivering, I shake violently, squeezing my hands into balls to protect my fingers. I shove them into my pockets, searching for warmth.

Beside me, Will is also freezing. His teeth are chattering so loudly, I can hear nothing else but the sound of bone clinking against bone. Several inches separate us, and I scoot to press up against him. I realize combining body heat is a useless feat when paired against a witch's magic, but my body moves on its own. I am responding on a cellular level to my mother's torture, and I have submitted to fight-or-flight responses.

"Enough! This is child's play," Abuela says. "Teach her a lesson, or I will."

The threat hangs heavy in the air, and I pray Mamá will not leave me to Abuela's anger. She will be vicious in her attacks, torturing me as she did Will. My grandmother will not stop until I beg her for mercy, and I cannot yield. I am too stubborn to grant her that. Together, we are a recipe for death and disaster.

The first time Mamá calls upon air, she uses it to whip me, but it does not hurt. It does not even leave a mark. I frown, wondering if the cold is playing tricks on my mind. Sadly, it is not. Mamá is holding back, and when it becomes obvious she is being lenient, Abuela loses her temper.

Furious, my grandmother uses her air magic to assault Mamá. It slams into her torso, and my mother shrieks. Trying to break her fall, she trips over her feet and lands on the ground in a fumbling heap. My grandmother's air magic moves her body with such ease, it is as if my mother were as empty and light as a tumbleweed on a hot, dry day.

My mother looks frail, weaker than I have ever seen her before. When I was a child, she looked so powerful, so formidable to me. As I would sneak around aimlessly in the night in search of souls we deemed evil, I feared her reaction. I never wanted her to discover my secrets, but I do not worry about that anymore.

As I look at her now, where she cowers on the ground beside me, I do not envy her position in this coven. Thanks to her mistreatment, there is a part of me—small but undeniably ruthless—that wants to ask her how it feels to be the center of this unwanted attention. I want her to glance my way, because I yearn to see that acknowledgment in her eyes. I want to witness the moment she recognizes that in the eyes of her high priestess, she has fallen to my level. I want to watch as she bears that truth.

But she does not look at me. With legs bent awkwardly beneath her, Mamá pushes herself upright and looks at my grandmother in disbelief. I wonder if this is the first time she has ever used her magic in anger before. I think about Holland's warning. Have they already gone mad? Perhaps I am too late. Maybe the darkness coursing through their veins already has its hold over them.

Abuela has never liked my mother—and she has never been shy about her feelings for her—but she tolerated her for Papá's sake. After he died, she was kind to her as a courtesy to me, the person she ordered to be the future leader of her coven. Now that the black magic has seeped into her pores, she is losing sight of what is right and what is wrong. I know I must stop this before she is too far gone.

"Stop!" I scream. "Can't you see what this magic is doing to you?"

Abuela faces me, her eyes so dark, they look black. Maybe they are. I do not know if it is the basement's dim lighting or if the dark magic has worked its way to her mind. Once it gains control, do the victims of black magic change appearances too? Will everyone who looks at her bear witness to its mark? I know too little about the black arts, and Holland seems light-years away from aiding me.

"You were always *weak*," Abuela says, spitting her words

at me with such shame and disgrace.

I fold under her accusation, her words worming their way into my heart. In true familial fashion, my grandmother knows just what to say to truly hurt me.

After Papá died, I admitted to her that I feared I would fall victim to a vampire too, that I would be too weak to survive an attack. I was young when I said this—too young to be showing signs of any *real* power—but now that I am older, when I think about the concerns I had back then, I wonder if I was already showing signs of spirit. Was my fear a vision? I had nightmares for years after Papá died, but Mamá said they were just the result of an overactive imagination. She doubted me—even then.

If only I could go back and comfort that young girl, I would tell her the truth about the people she loves. I would save her the greatest disappointment of her life—watching as she is forsaken by her coven for offering the very last thing she could to protect them: her mortality.

"I am not weak," I whisper.

"*¿Qué? ¿Qué dijiste?*" Abuela asks, seething. I know she heard me, but I repeat myself.

"*¡Dije que no soy débil!*" I scream.

A blast of air magic presses against my chest, and I am pushed upright. I skid against the ground, my jeans bunching at my bottom as I press against the dirt, trying to slow my progression backward. I am pushed back until my back is flush against the wall, and it sends a rush of fear through my entire body. My limbs stiffen, my mind spinning, and my blood is rushing behind my eyes.

The invisible force pinning me in place presses harder and harder against me, working its way up my torso, inch by inch.

It spreads like a fire, catching rapidly and stealing all sense of calm. My heart is pounding in my chest, and I fear it will break through my rib cage and plop onto the ground before me. I will simply stare at the bruised flesh, taking in my last gulps of life, while my grandmother laughs.

The magic she uses against me has reached my jaw now, and stretching my joints to their absolute limit, it pushes my head backward at an awkward angle until I hear a familiar crack. If Abuela pushes much farther, she will snap my neck clean off.

My limbs are held out beside me, with my left arm resting against Will. I cannot move. Frozen in place, I screech as the pressure becomes too much to bear. A final gasp, an instinctual reaction, releases the last bit of air in my lungs, and the magic compresses even tighter against my rib cage. Too tight within its grasp, I cannot breathe. I cannot suck in even a small gasp, and my body begins to convulse as it screams silently for oxygen.

I am dying. I know this to be true. I feel the agony of my body alerting me to this reality, even though I can do nothing to ease its suffering.

At the hands of my grandmother, I am dying, and everyone is just watching this happen.

"Stop!" Will shouts.

He grunts loudly as he pushes himself off the ground and charges my grandmother. Unfortunately, he is too weak, and she anticipated his devotion to me.

The moment she releases me, I fall to the floor, chest heaving as I gasp for air. It flows freely, my lungs sucking up oxygen so greedily, it is excruciating. I squeeze my eyes shut at the first painful sensation, and I hold my breath to make it stop. But that only makes my chest hurt more.

I know I must breathe slowly, but it hurts so bad, I do not even want to take a single gulp of air. Finally, when I cannot hold my breath any longer, I suck in a sharp burst. I hack, chest convulsing, and dig my nails into the dirt.

I suck in another breath. I taste grit, but I do not care. I welcome the grainy texture and earthy aroma, because it means I am alive. I survived. I am breathing, and I will be okay.

I open my eyes and try to blink away my blurry vision. It feels like a lifetime passes before I can see again. My chest calms, my breath comes in short, shallow streams. And I react to what is happening only feet away from me.

Finally, I see him. Will is across the room, screaming, as he takes the full brunt of my grandmother's fury. He is bleeding, with thick streams of dark crimson running down his face. His teeth are stained pink, and he spits up a sopping heap of something green and sticky. It coats his chin, splattering his already dirty T-shirt.

I scream. A brain-piercing bellow erupts from deep within my chest. I have no control over it or over the fear that engulfs me as I watch my grandmother murder Will. It is a screeching sound that would certainly send wolves running in the other direction.

I do not stop screaming until Abuela faces me, eyes flaring, chest heaving. Dimly lit by the light that dangles from the ceiling at the bottom of the steps, I see Abuela clearly. Her skin is pale, with black veins spreading like spider webs over her bony curves. As I look at her, squinting to ensure my mind is not playing tricks on me, I see it move, spreading farther, threading through her tissue until it connects again at the other side. It completely envelops her, flooding her with raw, dark power.

Realizing what is happening, that the dark magic is taking control, I scream, but this only angers her more. Her hands are balled into fists at her sides, and she throws one in my direction, fisting the air with her frustration over what I have done. I distracted her. I prevented her from killing Will. And she plans to make me pay for this.

Again, I am assaulted by her magic, but this time, I hear something snap in my chest. A sharp, stabbing pain erupts in my core, and I howl as the pain grows more violent with each passing second. I fight the agony, curling my body into a ball on the ground, waiting for Abuela to cease her brutal attack. I cradle my chest, shrieking when I irritate my wound as I hold on to my body, desperately trying to protect myself too tightly.

Deep within my core, I sense the darkness lurking. Where the vampire once resided, there is an emptiness, and it is hungry. It sparks to life, sizzling within my chest, and it feels eerily familiar to me.

The darkness hums, and the longer I focus on it—teasing, tempting, pulling it from where it slumbers—it begins to awaken. It swarms within me, threatening to expand until I can no longer contain it, but I hold on to it, using it to shield myself, to cocoon my body in its embrace. Its warmth washes over me, lingering on my freshly broken bones, and I feel as though they are mended. I jerk, shrieking as my ribs snap back into place. But the pain dulls quickly, and it is replaced by a hot, sticky hunger for vengeance.

My grandmother finally ceases her attack when the door to the basement opens, flooding the stairs with light. I dare a peek, watching as someone rushes downstairs and shouts something at my grandmother.

Time slows as I stare at Liv. Has she been here the whole

time? Has she heard my screams? Has she just listened as I begged for my grandmother to leave us be?

She looks at me, pity flashing behind her eyes, but the moment she notices my mother cowering on the floor, her pity is replaced by her resentment for all that I am. She believes I did this, and I do not correct her. I do not bother telling her that the enemy she must fear is the leader of this coven. She will soon discover that herself.

Liv rushes to Mamá, helping her to her feet, allowing my mother to rest against her small frame until she regains her composure and strength. Mamá does not look at me; she does not dare to witness what Abuela has done.

Commotion from upstairs catches my attention, but I look to Will, not caring about what the witches fear. I wonder if he feels the same darkness within him.

He is sitting upright, leaning against the wall. With the back of his hand, he wipes away the blood that cakes his nose and spits a mouthful on the ground beside him. In the darkness, it looks black. He sees it too and glances at me. His eyes are dark, his lids heavy, and I know he is on the brink of death.

Something flashes between us, a look of unity that we do not want to accept.

Because we both know we will not survive another night at the hands of these witches.

NINE

The witches are worried about something, and they are trying desperately to hide it from Will and me. They speak in frantic, hushed tones, but I sense their rising fear, their outrage. I want to listen closely, focus on their whispers, but all I can think about is how the burning agony in my side is suddenly only a dull ache.

Grunting, I sit up, back stiff, and instinctively clutch my side. I slide my hand underneath my jacket and grope my flesh, smoothing my palm over my wrinkled and stained T-shirt. The pain is almost completely gone.

But how is that possible? Did I heal myself?

I think about the events that led to this moment, completely ignoring the witches' banter as I assess my wounds. Abuela used her air magic against me, and the snap in my chest was all too real. I know I felt bone breaking, and that was only moments ago. How can it be mended now?

My grandmother's power formed a solid, impenetrable wall, and she used it to compress every inch of my torso. My bones gave way, something broke, and the pain radiated through me with a ferocity I have not experienced in months, thanks to my former vampire strength.

But now, as I press more firmly against my rib cage, the pain is gone.

Is it possible that the pit within me is not a void after all? I think about Mamá's words. She explained that the spell would sever my link to the vampire, but does that mean the vampire is truly gone? I cannot access its strength or heightened senses, and Mamá's spell was meant to leave only the witch. If I am the witch, then I am not powerless. I should still be able to summon magic. Maybe I was not trying hard enough. Maybe I just needed a little push—or, in my case, a little *compression*—to tap into my power.

My mind is spinning, my thoughts racing as I consider this newfound knowledge. I assumed I was tainted by this dark spell. I thought my magic was forever out of reach. It was so close, but I could not quite connect to it. I was beginning to think Mamá expected my reaction and used this specific spell to punish me.

But my magic was there, and unlike my assumptions, it was not simply to tantalize and remind me of days past. I just needed to stretch a little further in order to grab on to it. I just needed to believe in myself again.

Mamá hacks a wet, raspy sound that catches my attention, and I blink away the many thoughts swarming my mind. Still planted firmly on the ground where my grandmother left me, I look up at my mother. But she still does not look at me. I wonder if it is shame, embarrassment, or disgust that keeps her from meeting my gaze.

Mamá is walking beside Liv, and I find myself loathing my former best friend. She has never been better at choosing the most inopportune time to make her presence and distaste in me known. She judges me for my choices and believes the worst of me, even though she was never in my situation.

How can she know she would not have made the same

choices I did? I made mistakes, but I have always done what I thought was right. And the witches punish me for it. But no more. It is time I fight back.

"Perhaps we should bring our *guests* with us," Abuela says, breaking the silence. I hate the way she emphasizes *guests*, as if this is how she would actually treat someone she cherishes and respects.

A knot forms in my chest, clenching my heart so tightly I fear I will actually pass out. My mouth runs dry, my breath hitches. The darkness in my grandmother's voice is undeniable. Whatever is upstairs excites her to the point of risking our escape.

Slowly, Will and I ascend the stairs. He leans against me, offering more weight than I can handle. My forehead is damp, my chest heavy, as I carry weight for two up the long, narrow staircase.

When Will trips on a step, tumbling forward, I fall with him, fearing what will happen if he must catch his fall on his own. I let him slump against me, using my own arm to prevent smacking our foreheads against the sharp edges of the steps before us.

Will mumbles something under his breath—an apology, I think—but I ignore him. He does not need to apologize for the damage the witches have done. His embarrassment pains me.

Instead of responding, I help him up, letting him rest against me once again. I knew he was in bad shape, but I did not realize he was so cut off from his magic that he was not healing at all. Clearly, he has not experienced what I have, and I consider using the strength I have left to try to heal him.

I glance at Will and smile softly. He looks so different now. He is tall and lanky, his skin pale and taut. His hair is caked with dirt, his clothes are torn, and his eyes are dark and sunken. His body is bruised and bleeding, but his blood is not red. It is as black as the evil residing within him. I pray Holland will find a way to reverse this spell, because Will can only handle so much pain before he completely succumbs to it. And it is only a matter of time before I fall victim too.

Once again, we climb the steps, walking nearer to the bright, luminescent hallway ahead. Something about emerging above, joining the witches who await us, makes me nervous.

My heart is beating rapidly in my chest, and I am certain Will feels it. Our bodies are pushed up against each other as we work our way through the dozen or so unused coats that clutter the closet. When we emerge, the doorway to Will's basement prison slams shut behind us, and I jump at the sound.

Abuela is there, smiling at me, only inches behind us. Her eyes glimmer in the dim lighting, and her lips curve into a devious grin. It makes my blood run cold to see her be so... ruthless, so deranged, so unloving. Does she even realize how far gone she is?

She does not look at me the way a grandmother looks at her granddaughter or the way a high priestess looks at a young witch. I imagine she looks at me the way a hungry lion looks at a wounded gazelle. Somehow, I know I have only seconds before she feasts.

Will whispers something to me, and I glance up at him. I frown, giving him a puzzled expression. I was too busy worrying about my own problems to have heard his confession.

"I have...to sit," Will says softly.

I nod and look around, knowing I will find nothing acceptable for him to use. My grandmother will refuse him comfort, even as he sucks in his dying breath. I never knew she could be so cruel, but I am grateful to have seen this side of her. Once we make it out, there will be no going back for me. The witches are so desperate to sever something—why not our familial ties? Even if all I have is a dull, rusty hatchet, I will hack through those myself.

The house is nearly empty. Besides Abuela, Mamá, and Liv, there are only a few other witches. They watch us cautiously, far too eager to aid my former comrades should my grandmother give the ultimate order. I know we must be on our best behavior if we want to make it to nightfall.

I glance through the kitchen and out the window, hoping I can assess the time by seeing the sun's position, and I freeze.

Darkness has befallen Darkhaven. It is night. The moon is high in the sky. What happened to the sun? To the day? How long was I down there, trapped in time, succumbing to magical torture at the hands of my own blood?

I nudge Will with my shoulder and immediately regret my actions. He opens his eyes, still overly drowsy; his brief moment of reprieve was definitely not enough to dull the ache. I can tell his lids are still heavy even without truly looking at him. He needs food, water, rest—and he desperately needs a shower.

"It is night," I hiss. I never had a chance to divulge the plan with him. He was too busy trying to convince me that things could be worse. I snort at that thought, catching Mamá's glare.

"Come, children," Abuela says.

She leads us from the hallway, through the kitchen, and to the sliding glass doors. We step outside, finally witnessing what caused such a ruckus.

Several feet away, standing near our family altar, the

very one I have decorated so many times I have lost count, is Hikari. Her black pixie locks are slicked back, shiny against the moonlight. She is dressed in all black, and the sheath at her hip is empty. Her gaze darts from witch to witch, as if she is focusing intently on looking alert.

Another witch walks over to us and hands a sleek silver dagger with a wrapped black handle to my grandmother. I do not have to ask Hikari to know this is her weapon. It is almost identical to the one the others use. I assume this blade has brought many rogue vampires to their end, and now, my family intends to use it to send Will and me a message. Either we fall in line, or she will cast us out one final time.

I glance at my grandmother, understanding why she was so eager to allow us the opportunity to leave the basement dungeon. She stopped her physical assault only to cause emotional distress. She wants me to watch as she murders my friend. It is a scare tactic, and I know her well enough to know she plans to use this to ensure compliance. If she thinks murdering an innocent creature will convince me to obey her orders, then she truly has lost her mind.

"It seems you have a visitor, Ava," Abuela says. Her gaze averts from me to Hikari and then back again.

My grandmother grasps the handle of the dagger she has stolen and slaps the width of the blade against her other palm. She is waiting for me to respond, to acknowledge Hikari's presence, but I will not. Instead, I stare at my friend, my ally, who shakes under the gaze of so many formidable witches.

Hikari tries to stand tall, but being surrounded by her enemy, all mere seconds away from joining forces to summon the deadly elements, has an effect on her presence. Already petite, Hikari seems so much smaller. She looks...weak. I know she is not, but the witches are confident. There may not be a full coven here tonight, but they do not believe *one* vampire can outsmart them.

They are wrong.

"It seems your *friend* was going to rescue you," Abuela says. "Tell me, child, were you aware of her plan?"

Again, I do not answer. It does not matter what I say. If I admit that this was part of my plan to escape, I will be punished. If I say I did not know Hikari was going to come for me, Abuela will not believe me, and she will punish me for lying.

"Have you nothing to say?" my grandmother hisses, her anger tipping to the boiling point. She is seething, furious with my silence. She wants me to beg for my life, for Hikari's, but even I know that is a fool's dream. She will never grant leniency. She will never offer mercy. Our only way out is to fight for our freedom. But this we anticipated. Unfortunately, we did not expect my grandmother's ruthlessness.

A burst of air magic slams into my back, and Will and I fall forward. I should have expected her cheap shot, but I did not. We drop to the ground so quickly, I do not have time to break my fall—or Will's. Our faces smack against the frozen earth, but we land in a pile of fresh, soft snow.

I push myself up. Frantically shoveling away the fluff that buries my sick friend, I dig a path for Will to turn over. He hacks up more blood, and this time, when he spits it out, there is no denying its color. Thick, sticky, and black, the tarry substance that seeps from his mouth is definitely not blood. We stare at it in disbelief before he wipes away the evidence with the back of his hand.

"You are going to be okay," I whisper to him, praying I sound more confident than I feel right now.

"No, you will not," Abuela says. She stands behind us, a dark shadow lurking over our sunken frames. Even though I am certain it is impossible, we sink even farther into the ground as she stares down at us.

"*Por favor, Abuela. No hagas esto,*" I say, pleading with a clearly insane woman. My grandmother is too far gone—I know that. The black magic she cast has wormed its way into her head. Her skin is pale and veiny, with black streaks now almost completely covering her body.

How does no one else see what this magic is doing to her? Do they not understand that this will happen to them too? She succumbed first, but who will be next? I fear it will be Mamá, and I worry our link will ensure my demise as well.

"*Tuviste tu oportunidad. La desperdiciaste,*" Abuela says, grinding her teeth as she stares down at me.

"*¿Qué?* Are you serious?" I shout. "You never gave me a chance!"

A gust of air smacks into the side of my face, the bitter cold temperatures amplifying the pain. My grandmother struck me with her magic because she is too great a coward to use her hand. She smiles.

She wants me to lash out, to fight back. She wants me to prove to the others that I am no better than an animal worth putting down, as if I am some rabid beast intent on terrorizing this town. If they must fear someone, they should look at Abuela. But I know they will not, so I do not even try talking sense into them.

I clench my jaw shut, breathing heavily until my anger subsides. I am tired of being her punching bag, but I cannot ignite a war. Not tonight. Not until the moment is right. I may have Hikari by my side, but Will is still too weak to run, and I cannot carry him the whole way.

"*Defiéndete*," my grandmother orders, but I ignore her. I will not fight back. I will not give her the ammunition she needs to order the witches to kill Hikari. I know they will not stop at her. They will take out Will and me and anyone else who ever questions their orders.

"Perhaps your friend has better survival instincts," Abuela says as she steps back, granting Will and me much-needed space. I hear Will choke out a breath, and I try to help him up. I do not know which *friend* she means—Will or Hikari—so I fear for them both. I know Hikari can handle herself, so I assume Abuela is talking about Will, who clearly cannot withstand my grandmother's fury.

"This is what it has come to," Abuela says loudly.

I glance up at her, confused. She is no longer looking at me. She looks to the few witches who have come to her aid. I do not know where the others are. It is late, and I am certain Mamá and Abuela were not expecting a vampire attack so soon. Will and I are weak, and we were only taken captive recently. I suspect this is why the other coven members are at their own homes, resting peacefully tonight.

When they wake, they will discover the ambush. I wonder if they will feel it the way I did. Will they notice the exact moment their coven has been severed? Will they mourn their loss the way I miss being a vampire?

"These *abominations* are ungrateful," Abuela says. "We offered them renewed life, a sense of purpose, the opportunity to walk among us again, and they spit on us. They have no intention of rejoining us. Just today, I found my own granddaughter attempting to escape with our captive. The spell was supposed to unite us, but it is only pushing us further apart."

The other witches nod, and a few offer me piercing glares.

"They will never again be one of us," someone else shouts. I recognize her soft voice instantly.

I tear my gaze from my grandmother to meet Liv's eyes. In the moonlight, I see how much the black magic has affected her too. She looks frail beside the others. The moonlight illuminates her pale skin, emphasizing each bony curve. In the dark basement, I did not notice the spider web veins threading their way through her skin. They coat her arms and swarm up her neck. Unlike my grandmother's afflictions, Liv's have not quite reached her head, but I know they have pierced her heart. How else can she be so cruel?

I think back to the basement lighting. Was it enough to see her clearly? Were the marks there when we were in the dungeon? Or does this cancer move this quickly? Is this why Will is so sick? Until I saw the black tar spewing from his mouth, I thought he was merely hungry, thirsty, exhausted after days of torture, but clearly, something more is happening. He too is succumbing to the darkness.

I grab on to Will, holding him closely, as if my touch will keep away the monsters. I know it will not. This magic is far stronger and far darker than I predicted. If Holland still has not found a way to reverse the spell, I fear we will not survive.

"We must rid the world of them—once and for all," Abuela says before she looks down at me.

She is only a few feet away, and already, her face betrays her inner desire. She faces no turmoil, no fear. She does not care that she is telling these people—most who do not know me—to kill me. I understand why the witches are so prejudiced against that which they do not understand. They fear it, and they raise their young to fear the same things. My only hope was to escape this vicious cycle.

My grandmother takes a step toward me, Hikari's dagger tight within her grip, and a million different ways she can kill me flash before my eyes. I do not have the protection of heightened senses or superior strength to keep me safe, and I wonder if she planned this all along. Did she ever intend to give me a chance at a new life? Or was it always her intention to eliminate her burden by removing me from Darkhaven completely?

Her fingers tease the black fabric strap of the dagger in her hand, her nails scratching at it as she smiles down at me. My pulse is rising, my breath coming in short, shallow bursts. I try to think of a way to escape, but every scenario playing in my mind ends the same way.

We all do not make it out alive.

I glance at Will, who smiles at me with sleepy eyes. Sometimes, when he looks at me, I feel like he can read my mind. We both understand how dire our situation is. We both understand it is kill or be killed, but everyone knows we do not have the strength or the numbers to survive this fight.

At least, that is what Hikari and I want the witches to believe.

I panic, making a show of my emotions. I breathe heavily, shrieking for my mother to save me. Deep down, in the very center of my heart, it stings to ask this of her, because I know she will refuse me. She does not even look my way when I beg for my life, and that reality hits me—hard.

Every time I think this is the moment I will remember forever, this is the moment my former coven has pushed too far, *this* is the moment my life is over due to the depraved actions of my family, they do something else even more vicious, even more spiteful, even more malicious. It hurts me to know I am related to such vile beings.

"How can you do this to me?" I say, letting the tears flow freely. I do not have to pretend anymore. The pain of her actions root deeply in my gut.

I think about all the times I fought for them. I defended them. I offered my life and my soul to protect them, and every chance they got, they tried to take me down. Amicia once told me these witches do not deserve my loyalty, and my biggest regret is not ruining my relationship with my family by asking a vampire to turn me into one.

My biggest regret is the moment I did not listen to the vampires when they warned me about the malicious actions of my own people. I was a fool who believed in peace and love, hope and prosperity. I believed the next generation deserved more than *this*. They deserve more than some pointless feud destined to end in nothing but death.

"I believed in you even when you refused to believe in me," I whisper, looking at Mamá, thinking about all the times I begged the vampires to give the witches a chance.

"*¿Qué dijiste?*" my grandmother asks, but I ignore her. I do not repeat myself, because she knows exactly what I said. Besides, I am not talking to her anymore.

"I prayed you would see through your prejudice and just accept what I have become, but I see now that you cannot," I say. "You are *toxic*. I will not sacrifice myself for you anymore."

I understand now that becoming a vampire was never a curse. Vampirism was the antidote for the poison that is the very people who gave me life.

"I do not regret turning my back on you, Mamá, or leaving this coven. I only regret that it took me this long to see the truth, to remove your mask and unveil the monster residing within your soul."

"*¡Cállate!*" my grandmother yells. She throws out her arms, and I shield my face, prepared to protect myself from her weapon or her magic, whichever she plans to use to silence me.

Except it never comes.

Someone screams, and I jerk my head away, ignoring my grandmother. I blink and Hikari is no longer by the altar. She dodges a witch's attack, effortlessly twirling through the air. The fireball meant to kill her slams into a nearby snow mound, turning the icy frost into a steaming pool.

Hikari is running, but she is running closer to Mamá's house and farther from the woods, from where her allies await her. She bypasses several witches, evading all of their attacks. I think she is coming for me, but this is not part of the plan.

When she and Malik covered the details with me, they never explained this part. Hikari was to be a decoy, so where are the others? Does she plan to simply grab my hand and run? What about Will? Can she carry us both to safety? If we leave without him, returning to experience the witches' magical torture was for nothing.

I cannot leave without him. No, I *will not* leave without him. With my eyes, I try to convey this to Hikari, who is steadily running toward me, but she never meets my gaze.

She moves so quickly, she looks like she is flying, though I know she is not. She glides through the air like an angel soaring through the heavens, and when she lands on the ground again, her feet plop into the snow quietly. The witches are frantically casting spells and summoning their magic, desperate to stop her pursuit. I wonder if they too believe she is coming for me.

A knot forms in my gut, because I do not know what she

is doing. But I know she is not coming for me. I wait, with bated breath, as my tired senses try to keep up with her swift movements.

The moment Hikari is by her side, I understand her intentions. I suck in a sharp breath, but I fall silent. Internally, I am screaming. I do not want her to die, because I do not know what her death will mean for *him*. I am scared, terrified of the cost. But I understand, without being involved in the discussion that made this choice; they need to experiment, to attempt to sever this link by force. To accomplish that, they need a volunteer, knowing they could never ask for one.

Hikari is by her side before the witches understand what she is doing, for they do not have all the pieces. But I do. I remember the look of fear in Malik's eyes when he told me Holland informed him of our chat. He knew about the link to Mamá, and he understood the path I was on. I did not have to tell him how dark magic worms its way into a person's sanity and roots itself there, stealing her rationality.

I know I asked too much of Holland. Unfortunately, he did not witness the spell, and I know far too little about black magic to save my soul. This was Malik's only option; I know that. But it does not replace my agony or my fear.

I have only seconds to make a decision. Either I remain silent or I stop Hikari from committing an irreversible act. I know I must decide quickly, but my brain is tired, my mind fuzzy, my body weak. I am exhausted from magical torture and chilled by the brutal outside wind. My hands are so cold they are becoming stiff, and my mouth is dry, my tongue a useless husk. The part of my brain that must make quick decisions is stalling, the receptors frozen in place.

I hold Will's hand, but I do not look at him. I do not want

to see his reaction. I do not want to know if he understands what is about to happen. Because Will is Malik's experiment.

Hikari reaches for her with pristine accuracy. She flips in the air, landing swiftly behind her. I do not see the moment Hikari's hands grab on to her skull, and I do not notice them twisting until the witch's neck snaps.

But I know this happens, because she is falling.

A moment of silence passes. The world is so still and moving so slowly, all I can hear is the quick inhalation that we all take in unison. No one expected this, not even me. I believed Malik when he explained the plan, and I never wondered if he might be hiding something that he was certain I could not handle.

She falls to her knees first. Her limbs stab into the snow, sinking deeply, rooting her body in place like some cruel, disgusting piece of art. Her torso falls next, and she lands at the perfect angle.

After she falls, her body is illuminated in a patch of moonlight. Her dark-brown hair is shiny under its rays, and her skin looks soft and pale. Only the faint black lines swirling around her exposed skin remind me that she is not the girl I once knew. She was changed. She was evil. They stole her innocence and replaced it with a monster.

The moment of silence ends, the shock finally settling, and the world erupts into screams. The unfamiliar witches to me must have known her well, because the agony piercing the silent night is surely enough to awaken every sleeping citizen of Darkhaven, even those not privy to what lurks in the night.

I cannot tear my gaze away from her, and when I finally do, it is because someone is at my side. It is Will. I hear his voice, but his words are muffled. He is shaking me. He cups my face, forcing me to look away, tearing my gaze from her body.

Only then do I realize it is me who is screaming, mourning the loss of someone supposed to be so pure.

Tears flood my vision. They stream down my face, turning icy in the bitter night air. Finally, as I blink away my pain, falling numb to the events of tonight, I look into Will's eyes, and three things become abundantly clear.

First, Liv is dead. Hikari killed her.

Second, the crimson irises staring back at me are Will's.

Third, I understand now what I must do.

I tell myself not to be afraid. I remind myself Mamá put herself in this position when she cast that spell. She dabbled in the black arts and condemned her soul to eternal darkness. She did so willingly. She ripped the vampire from my body, leaving a gaping wound in its wake, and never cared about the repercussions or what losing part of myself might do to me.

I look at my mother, and she stares back at me defiantly. She understands as well. Will's link to Liv severed the moment she died, and this only means one thing.

My freedom will only come with Mamá's demise.

TEN

Magic makes a crackling sound when it is harnessed. The more powerful the witch, the louder the sound. When I listen for it, I think of corn combusting and maracas shaking to my favorite beat.

And I hear it now. It sounds like firecrackers cast into the darkened sky. Sometimes, it even sparkles like fireworks, illuminating the witch's soul with bright, shiny, iridescent rays of pure, raw energy.

Magic surrounds us. The witches are outraged, and they intend to avenge their fallen. I expect nothing less. I committed these very acts of vengeance numerous times in the name of protection. Of course, I was protecting *them*, avenging *them*. They only wish to harm *me*. So it is not quite the same thing.

Still, the picture of violence is erupting all around me, and I can do nothing to stop it. I cannot even aid my allies. I am far too weak to use force against the witches, and even if I had the strength to fight, I am certain they would outmatch me with the flick of a wrist. I am no match for the elements. At this point, I can barely call upon one myself.

Flashes of light pierce my vision, and I squeeze my eyes shut, hoping the flames will soon turn to embers, but they never relent. When I worry this act is making me too vulnerable under the circumstances, I partly shield my eyes with my hand and take a peek.

The witches and their fire magic are unforgiving. I look around, unable to move from where I am rooted. The havoc of war is everywhere. All I see is death and blood, and all I hear are screams and the methodical swish of metal piercing the air. One by one, my enemies fall.

Still a few feet from my mother, I do not look at her any longer, and she does not look at me. I do not have to peer at her to know this. I no longer feel the pinprick of eyes gazing at my back.

Instead, I feel a rumbling thunder in my heart, and it flows into my body through my feet. It hammers at the frozen tundra before me and radiates from my soles through my limbs. The sensation makes me shudder as it cascades against my bones. A formidable sound I am all too familiar with, it makes me uncomfortable.

I know what this sound is, and it is not coming from me, nor is it coming *for* me.

In the distance, I watch them approach. My saviors are here to aid their comrades. Dressed in black, they blend in perfectly with the dark, foggy woods beyond my mother's property. When they emerge from the shadows, where they awaited Hikari's signal, the silver of blades strapped to their waists glisten in the moonlight. They run in unison, the amber glow of fire magic already spotlighting their approach.

The moment my gaze falls upon Jasik, my heart swells. My eyes are moist, and I suck in a sharp breath. Regardless of Malik's promises to me, I still feared I would never see my sire again. Even a day away from him felt like a lifetime of his absence.

Somehow, even with the vampire severed from the witch,

I simply feel stronger when Jasik is near. It is as if his inner strength fortifies my own. Together, I imagine we can become an unstoppable duo. We just need a chance to become one.

I break my gaze and silently thank the other hunters. Malik knew he needed time to convince Amicia of the importance of saving Will. I thought he did this as a courtesy to me, and perhaps, deep down, that was part of the reason he agreed to assist me. After all, we are family now. If not to help each other, what are families for? I certainly will not be asking the witches this anytime soon.

But I know Malik separates his emotions from what must be done. No one else is better at replacing pain with righteousness. He would sacrifice his own life if his death needed to happen. That is just the kind of man he is.

I envision him explaining to Amicia the dire consequences I am in. This spell not only affects me, but it will irrevocably alter every witch who participated in its casting. And that affects Darkhaven. The vampires may reside here in secrecy, living their days by hiding in the woods, but it will not be long before the aftermath of this dark spell reaches even their doorsteps. Are the vampires prepared for that? I guess Amicia did not think so.

I wonder if Amicia knew the parts of the plan I did not. Did Malik tell her he planned to sacrifice Will as part of his experiment? Did he tell Jasik or Jeremiah? Did everyone but me know the toll this fight will have on my life?

I tear my vision from the vampires in search of Will. He aids the vampires, enacting his revenge against those who tortured him for the past two days. I watch as his fist thrashes forward, and a witch falls, her body lifeless as she takes her final breath. It echoes in my mind, and I am certain this is only my imagination playing tricks on me. I do not have the heightened senses to truly hear her breathe.

No longer weakened by the spell that clung to his life force, Will has been rejuvenated. His body is flush with color, his irises are swirling crimson, and his muscles bulge from beneath his clothes.

Will fights with strength I cannot fathom. He runs at speeds I almost cannot see. It feels as though decades have passed since I last felt that *rush* of power. The vampire feels so far gone, yet so close I can practically taste her desire for bloodshed. She is angry. She wants vengeance too. And I desperately want to give it to her. I want to succumb to the darkness, shut off my emotions and just *live*.

But at the cruelest of times, I am reminded that I am no longer a vampire. Like when my friends fight my battles, and I must simply watch and hope they make it through.

The night is cold, and a sharp wind blows through the forest, rattling the bare branches. The blast of air is so harsh, it swarms my mind, allowing me to hear nothing else. I suppress a shiver and try to stand. I need to move, to take cover. Unlike the vampires, I cannot withstand the bitter temperatures. My clothes are wet and tattered, and the air burns against my exposed skin.

I try to trek through the snow, trying to stay low, stay safe, just stay *out of the way*. But all around me, there is carnage and fireballs and screams. I try not to listen, because I know these sounds will haunt me until the day I die. For that reason alone, I am thankful Mamá's spell cut my life short. I do not need these visions or these cries for help to follow me for an eternity.

I am standing, spinning in a circle, unsure of where to go,

where to hide. Thankfully, no one notices me. I suppose that is the only perk of this spell. Not considered a threat, I have become invisible. But my enemies are not so lucky.

The vampires effortlessly evade the witches' attacks. The sound of metal scraping against bone makes my stomach queasy, so I try not to focus too intently on the chaos surrounding me.

I turn 'round and 'round, searching for a safe place to wait out the storm, but I succeed in only dizzying myself. I try to take a step forward but trip over something solid, and I shriek as I plummet to the ground. Already icy and stiff, my hands begin to scream at me.

Something catches my eye, and when I turn my head, I stare into the lifeless eyes of Liv, my best friend. I suck in a sharp, cold gasp. Regardless of what happened, tears prickle at my eyes, and I am grateful for the wave of pain washing over me. My torment over losing her means the spell has not quite clutched my sanity the way it has the others. At least not yet, but I know I do not have much time.

Liv's eyes are still open, as if she was just as surprised as I was when Hikari targeted her. Already, her eyes are turning murky in color. Her pupils are cloudy, but her irises are black, not the chocolate-brown color I remember them to be.

I hate that she died while under the influence of black magic, but it gives me comfort to know her death was quick, painless, and I assume that was Hikari's gift to me. She does not want me to hate her for killing my friend, but part of me does anyway. The part of me that still believes it is crazy to live like this—in constant fear of yet another fight brewing between the witches and the vampires—wants to go back in time and save Liv, but I am no wizard.

Liv's skin is pale, and her lips are blue. She is cold, her skin icy as a fresh layer of snow scatters her body. I brush away what has coated her neck and peer at her skin. The black veins that were encroaching her jawline seem higher now. Is it possible they are still moving? Or do they spread that quickly?

Guilt washes over me, and I drown in it. I choke out a cry and brush hair from Liv's face, but I succeed in only smearing something over her skin. With tears in my eyes, I try to wipe it away but only manage to make a bigger mess. Confused, I look at my hands and suck in a sharp breath. My palms are covered in that same black, tarry substance that Will and Mamá hacked out earlier.

The darkness is inside of me. It is happening. Now.

I sit back, resting my bottom on the soles of my feet. My butt is cold, and the caked snow on my shoes does not help to alleviate the chill. The snow has seeped through my jeans now, and my shins are freezing. The frigid temperatures drop steadily as night envelops the village, and the breeze tousles my hair.

Frantically, I try to wipe off the substance by wiping my hands together, but it does no good. It is still there. Quickly, afraid if I wait too long this substance will seep into my pores, I pile snow onto my hands and use it to clean myself, but still, it does not remove the tar.

Breathing heavily, I feel my anxiety rising. My heart is screaming, my mind becoming hazy as blood rushes to my brain. I scrape my palms against my thighs, certain this will remove it. Again, it does not.

I shriek as I stare at my hands, and the tar moves, taking on a life of its own. Quickly, it spreads, fanning out, wrapping around my hands and shooting up my arms. I feel it everywhere.

Without even seeing myself, I know I am cocooned by it. I am one giant blob of black tar, and no one seems to notice.

How is this happening right now?

I feel the substance penetrate my flesh, and when I scream again, it floods my mouth. I choke on it. It tastes like rotting flesh. It is gritty and thick, and it swarms within me, buzzing as it fills even the deepest crevices of my body. It is everywhere inside of me, blending seamlessly with me on a cellular level. It takes over, and I have no idea where it ends and I begin.

I am screaming, but when I search the yard, desperate for Jasik or Will or anyone who actually cares about me, I see only Liv and the countless unfamiliar witches who have died because of me, because of this endless war.

The witches are angry, throwing out their arms, blasting their elemental magic at me. It slams into my chest, burning straight through to my core.

I do not look down. I do not want to see the result of the witches' hatred. But I do not have to look at my wounds to know I feel hollow, like the very center of my body has been fried away.

I think I am dying. I am light-headed, my vision blurry, and my heartbeat begins to slow. Is this what it feels like to die? I died once, and it was excruciating. The transition from witch to vampire was brutal because my senses were rapid firing. All at once, I could hear, see, taste, smell, feel...*everything*. But this time, it is different. Cut off from my senses, I am plummeting into oblivion. Never in my life have I been so terrified of darkness.

I pray I am dreaming. That thought cradles me in warmth and safety. Maybe I am in my bed, safely tucked away deep inside the manor. I am surrounded by vampires, in the one place the witches cannot reach me. Maybe everything so far was just a dream, and when I wake, I will be a vampire again. I will be happy, healthy, strong.

When the thought occurs to me that I might not be in the manor, that I might still be in the basement, I nearly black out from the rush of fear. Maybe this is my grandmother's cruel trick. Maybe she is using the black magic to penetrate my mind, to make me see things that are not really there.

Maybe it is too late. Maybe I am too far gone to be saved.

"Ava!" someone screams.

I feel Will grab on to my arms. His long fingers wrap around my flesh, holding firmly, and he shakes me. My body is stiff and does not give way easily. I fight against him, wanting him to just go away. I want this to stop. I want all of it to just be over. I cannot take much more of these games.

I remind myself that Will was with me in the basement too. He might still be there with me, suffering brutal treatment at the hands of those who pledged to protect this town.

He screams my name over and over again, but I do not want to open my eyes. I do not want to see his eyes any other color but crimson. I want to know he is strong and safe and that we are one quick run from escaping captivity.

When he lets go of me and releases a loud grunt, I finally open my eyes. Will no longer shouts my name. He is not holding on to me, desperate for me to awaken. In fact, he is not beside me at all. Will is soaring through the air.

For a brief moment, the world stills as I watch him flutter away.

Then he comes crashing down, slamming into Jeremiah, who was fighting off another witch's attack. Will lands clumsily, and they fall into a tangled heap. Both frantically trying to stand, they scramble for far too long, and another witch is swiftly approaching, her hand already raised to call upon her magic.

I look at my own palms, and the tar is gone. I turn over my hands, assessing my skin. It is smooth and clear and clean. The black veins that penetrated me so deeply are no longer there.

I was imagining it all. I am still free, but only if I keep moving. I must keep moving.

I look at Liv, and her lifeless eyes still carry their accusations, so I shovel snow onto her face, burying her beneath the rubble. I do not want to look at her anymore. She decided her fate the moment she aided the witches in my demise. I must remember that. We are not at fault for her mistakes.

On shaky legs, I stand. My stomach churns at what I see. All around me, witches are falling. The vampires are taking no prisoners, and I know I should not mourn the deceased—they all had it coming—but it pains me to know *this* is what it has come to. My release only comes with their death.

An ear-splitting shriek penetrates the night air, and the sound rips through my heart. I scan the yard in search of the victim, my gaze settling on one of my few allies. My blood runs cold, the icy air no longer burning my weakened skin.

Hikari is on her knees, and she is clutching her side. Trying to stand, she moves her hand, betraying a long slash across her torso. She is surrounded by three witches. They encircle her, their arms at their sides as they summon the elements.

I freeze. I am not surprised the witches would target her. Our enemies are vengeful by nature, but I refuse to let Hikari fall simply because she was trying to save *me*.

I know she only has moments to make a move, or she will

succumb to their power. I must think quickly. *How* can I aid her? I remember the moment I used magic to heal myself. I was pinned against the floor, brutalized by my grandmother, and something within me just...snapped. The power swelled, and I released it, using it to heal my broken bones.

Instinctively, I reach for my side. The pain is still gone. My wounds are still closed. If I can summon enough magic to simply distract the witches, maybe the others can dash to her side. Or maybe enough time will pass for Hikari to save herself.

I squeeze my hands at my sides, pumping my fists, tightening my core. Deep down, I feel my magic springing to life. Unlike the usual waterfall ferocity, it is slow-moving, and I fear too much time will pass before I am able to channel enough strength to help Hikari.

The witches are raising their arms now, chanting so quickly, I can barely hear the spell they are casting. She has only seconds. It is now or never.

My chest is heaving, my lungs pumping oxygen to the rest of my body in rapid bursts of gassy energy. My limbs burn as the fire in my gut rises into my chest. I am reaching my boiling point, and I know I must release this magic soon or I might actually combust.

At the exact moment that I am certain I can no longer contain my magic, I throw my arms out before me and scream, releasing every bit of agony I had pent up. A solid flow of anger and pain and fear bursts from my palms as fiery streams of liquid magic. The lava substance shoots across the yard, aiming unevenly at the witches surrounding Hikari.

I miss.

Having spent far too many days not practicing magic, I misjudge the distance, and I almost set Hikari on fire.

Thankfully, my emotional duress caught the attention of everyone in the yard, giving Hikari enough time to leap away. She twists through the air, landing lightly on her feet several yards away.

Seeing how Hikari is no longer in the cross hairs of three powerful witches, I lower my arms and slump forward, nearly tripping over my feet as I try to catch my breath. I am weak, desperate for nutrition and rest but believing I am likely hours away from relief. If it even comes at all.

As my stammering heart slows to a comfortable level, I glance up and assess our situation. The vampires are winning, and things are not looking good for Mamá's coven or for the unfamiliar allies she has assembled to murder us. The vampires might not have the numbers the witches have, but they are far greater predators. It is only a matter of time before they eliminate them all.

Just when I consider Mamá might recognize this herself and ask her coven to retreat, she does the unthinkable.

I feel the exact moment her fingers wrap around the back of my neck. I can barely breathe. Her fingers squeeze so hard I almost pass out, but as soon as I become light-headed, she loosens her grip just enough to keep me conscious.

The point of her blade teases the throbbing vein in my neck, and I wince as the metal digs deep enough to cut me. The thick substance dripping down my neck tickles my skin as it descends until it seeps into the fabric of my jacket, halting its retreat.

"Stop!" my mother screams, her voice ragged and raspy. She is so close to my ear, it is painful when she speaks. "Retreat or I will kill her!"

I do not move, terrified that even a tiny flinch will make

her dig her blade even deeper into my flesh. My arms dangle at my sides as I stand straight enough to make my back ache. I am shaking. I try to calm my nerves so I do not tremble so violently that I cut myself.

My heart sinks as I work up the courage to look from one vampire to the next. They look from my mother, who stands directly behind me, to where her weapon is cutting my neck. A look of confusion crosses their faces as they consider what is being asked of them.

But no one moves, because like me, even the vampires are unsure of what to do. The witches still as well, awaiting orders.

I scan my enemies' faces, finally settling on Abuela. She smiles at me, and I notice, unlike the rest of her coven, she is completely unharmed. My grandmother is standing by the glass doors that lead to the kitchen, close to where she was when she brought Will and me outside to meet our fate. Instead of joining this fight, she watched as she ordered others to their demise.

I narrow my eyes at her, but this only pleases her more. Her eyes sparkle with joy, and a hint of bile works its way into my throat, forcing me to look away.

Malik planned this night perfectly. I would be captured, and I would locate Will. The next evening, Hikari would be sent to scout the area, intentionally getting caught. The witches would gloat, assuming the frail-looking Hikari was not a threat, and they would force me to watch as they kill her. At that moment, the vampires would make their presence known, revealing their intentions all along.

Even if I was left in the dark for much of his plan, Malik described this night so accurately it was as if he already lived it himself. He anticipated every move—except for this one.

Who would have believed my mother would be so deranged, so afflicted by the darkness within her, that she would threaten to slice my neck with her own hand?

They could not have foreseen this moment, and now, they are not sure how to proceed. Do they retreat, or do they fight, risking my life? They look to me for instruction, but even I do not know what to do. Either way, I feel doomed.

"Mamá," I whisper, a single tear sliding down my cheek.

Again, I ask myself, how has it come to this? How are we here right now? How is Mamá capable of *murdering* me? As much as I hate her for what she has done, Tatiana is still my mother. I could not intentionally harm her so fiercely she *dies*. I would never forgive myself if it were *my* blade that resulted in her death.

My mother responds by squeezing my throat tighter. It is a warning. She will do what she must to protect the remaining members of her coven, even if that means murdering her child. She feels cornered, and maybe killing me is her only way out.

Thanks to Liv's sacrifice, we understand that our link is severed at death, but not at life. Will and Liv both were succumbing to the darkness inside of them, courtesy of that link. Now, that darkness remains within Liv, and Will is free. But when they were linked, he experienced her agony. That darkness tortured them both.

So what does that mean? My mind is spinning as I think about that fateful night. Mamá linked herself to me, joining us as one. Even when I was back with the vampires, I still felt her essence inside me. She was *always* there, taunting me.

Honestly, it was no different than my childhood. As I grew up, she constantly reminded me how inferior my magic was to hers. Never taking me seriously or believing my instincts, she made me believe she was always more powerful. Because she was. Mamá can summon the elements quicker than any witch I have ever met. She truly is a force to be reckoned with.

I still, freezing slightly. Mamá does not seem to notice, but I am certain the vampires do. Jasik frowns, his gaze focused solely on me. He is looking for a clue, for some secret message as to what he should do. He thinks I have a plan, and unfortunately, I do. But it is one I must complete on my own. The vampires cannot save me, but I can save myself.

Fearful I will back out and submit to the witches, I do not give my plan much thought. Instead of thinking things through, I live in the moment, risking everything I have ever known on the fact that Mamá was always right.

I have always believed that Mamá was more powerful than me, but that was before I became a vampire. Now, severed from my vampire half, she is once again better, stronger—but she is not smarter.

I close my eyes and whisper a strengthening chant. I feel the fire in my gut grow stronger at the mere sound of the familiar incantation. It is not enough to save me tonight, but it is enough to remind myself of how powerful a single witch can be.

But thankfully, and courtesy of Mamá's plan to bring me home as a witch, not a hybrid, I am not just *one* being. Not anymore. Mamá is not simply a powerful spirit witch; she is also royalty. I was supposed to one day lead this coven, but without me around, that burden falls to my mother. Mamá is the rightful heir, and that gives her power. That makes her connected to *them*, to an entire coven of witches.

I imagine this is why Abuela did not volunteer herself as tribute when someone needed to be tied to Will and me. She knew tethering herself—the high priestess of a coven—would offer too powerful a link. What she did not consider is my mother's relationship to her.

Mamá is her daughter by marriage, not blood, but magic does not discriminate. During Papá and Mamá's handfasting ceremony, where they pledged eternal love and loyalty to each other, they exchanged blood—becoming one, essentially. This is a great misjudgment on Abuela's part, and I will use it against her.

The spell that linked me to my mother formed something between us. This bond flows freely, and it is alive with power. I sense it when my eyes are open, but when I close them, I can *see* it. It is swirling with vibrant colors, encompassing both of us together...as one.

I reach through that link, forcing my own essence into Mamá. When I reach her power swirling within her, I use it to strengthen my own innate magic. I may have been too weak to properly aid Hikari, but now I am overflowing with power.

After the spell was completed, Mamá kept reassuring me that I am a witch now. That the spell severed my vampire half, leaving the witch to become the dominant species. But that does not mean the vampire is *gone*.

I know she is there, in the darkness, waiting, watching, lurking. I feel her hunger, her desire. Courtesy of that spell, the vampire has been *silenced*, and I think it is time I return her voice.

When I pull Mamá's essence back into me, using the same portal she was using to torment me only hours ago, I feel rejuvenated with strength. And I use that energy to fill the gap inside of me. Magic cascades down upon that dark abyss, showering it with light, and finally, I see her. The vampire.

The spell the witches cast did not remove her. They simply suppressed her, just as they assured me they would do.

Surging with power, I chant, silently, calling the elements to aid me now. I sense the exact moment I come into power. Not because I hear the distinct crackling sound that betrays the use of magic or because I feel the surge of power, but because the outside world changes. The weather warms, and a fine mist settles over the land. The snow at my feet begins to melt as the elements encompass me. My body radiates the heat that warms me from the inside out.

Mamá gasps, and I feel the wound on my neck sizzling until it closes. I know I am healed. Closing my wound was not my intention, but I am bubbling with power. It is seeping through my pores, closing wounds as it completely consumes me.

Understanding what is happening, Mamá quickly withdraws her hand, striking my flesh with the sharp edge of her blade. She wishes to silence me, to cease my attack, but my wound heals quickly.

My body is shaking, and I am growing tired. I can only tap into this power and hold on to this magic for so long, and soon I will burn out. Unlike my former coven, I will not contain magic not meant to be mine. I will release it, but for now, I have just enough at my disposal to make one final declaration against the witches.

I know what I must do, but I understand it comes at a terrible cost. If things were different, if I were able to draft a plan with consideration just as Malik had, I might make different choices right now. Unfortunately, I do not have time to consider my options. I must act. Now.

I open my eyes and throw my arms out to my sides.

The wind changes as I shout my incantation at the world. Intentionally, I speak rapidly, hoping the elemental assault I am releasing upon the witches is distracting them enough to disorient them. The last thing I want is for them to understand my spell and then reverse it.

Mamá screams, and though I do not see her, I know she is no longer standing at my side. She has withdrawn her weapon, and I am safe, protected by the magic she used to threaten me with all those years ago.

The elements surge all around me, swirling viciously as they tear through the flesh of those who attempt to stop me. It will not relent.

Realizing there are not enough witches here to stop me, the witches are forced to watch, helplessly, as I steal every last bit of their magic. Their power is in their life's blood, and I am sucking it from them, leaving behind nothing but the mundane.

I summon the moon, using her power to strengthen my spell, and she aids me feverishly, as though she has missed my nightly call. I have missed her too, and I know, when I am done and the spell has been cast, I will miss it even more than I do now. Because there is no going back. I will never again call upon her in this way. Our connection will be broken by my own hands.

This spell is their punishment—and mine too. But I welcome it as my retribution for the many evil acts I have committed over my years hunting vampires. I do not think about how many innocents I have killed in the name of honor and protection. I accept my fate. This is the moment I take back my life, but in doing so, I must make my greatest sacrifice.

I scream at the wind, squeezing my eyes shut as I shout. It now howls loudly all around us, and I can barely hear my own voice.

I open my eyes, watching as the witches are swept away, succumbing to the fury of the elements. They fall to the ground, writhing, as the pieces of them that contain magic are ripped from their very souls. I will not deny that it brings me joy to know they are experiencing the pain they have caused me.

The vampires stand in awe, unaffected by the spell that was not cast for them. I glance at Will, who looks on, a deep crease in his forehead, because unlike the others, he understands the cost of such a powerful spell. But this is all I have. This is all I can do to protect myself, to end this feud once and for all. To me, that cost is worth my life.

When the spell has been cast and the world stills, I fall to my knees, relinquishing my hold over the elements. The magic I harnessed seeps back into the earth, tucking away, always near but forever out of reach.

My heart is racing, my chest heaving, as I try to catch my breath. With the witches also experiencing similar agony, the vampires sheath their weapons. I do not need to announce that the battle is finally over for them to realize these witches are no longer a threat to us.

Jasik rushes to my side, and I smile at him when he squats down beside me.

"It is over," I whisper.

He frowns, not understanding the ramifications of what I just did, but I do. Will does. Holland will too. We will go home now, and I will tell him and the others what they can expect of me. I know they will be upset with me for casting a spell with such...finality. But they will forgive quickly with the intention of cherishing what little time we have left.

Jasik helps me up, and I lean against him, burying my head against his chest as he wraps his arms around me. I relish in his scent, in his embrace, knowing nothing will ever be the same between us.

When I look up at him, he kisses my forehead softly. When he pulls back, I still feel the cool press of his lips against my skin. He stares at me, his crimson irises burning brightly, and I know, even though I am fully aware that I will never be the same girl he once treasured, he somehow still sees me as that strong, confident girl he saved so many moons ago. He still sees me as the vampire, and I will cherish that until I take my final breath.

Because I am not that vampire. Not anymore. Even though I yearn to be her once again. Things are different now, and life will never be the same.

I slide my palm against Jasik's. He threads his fingers between mine, and a tingling sensation hurls up my arm. I feel like I have not been close to him in *months*, even though I know that is not true. I glance over my shoulder, turning to face her.

My mother is on the ground, and she stares up at me in disbelief. I am not sure what surprises her more—the fact that I was smart enough to think of this spell, or the fact that I was able to harness that much power and use it against them. She always assumed me to be weak, so I will guess it is the former that shocks her. Really, I should thank her. Without the black magic she used to cast her own dark spell, I would never have thought to create one of my very own making.

"How?" she whispers.

Already, the feeling of emptiness should be washing over her, and I cannot help but smile. I wonder how she will survive that void, the dark pit in her gut that threatens to consume her.

"You have always doubted me, Mamá," I say. "You never believed I was strong enough or smart enough to best you, but I proved that I am."

Jasik squeezes my hand, his silent signal that we must return home. He believes the witches will recover, and violence will erupt once again, breaking the peace. But it will not. For now, the feud is over.

"I committed the very same act against you, Mamá, that you did to me. I used your spell and harnessed *good* energy from the moon and from the vampire to strengthen it," I explain without divulging too much information. I would not want their purgatory to end too quickly.

"But..." She trails off, her gaze darting between me and the other witches who cower behind me. I do not even worry about them. Finally, I am not afraid.

"You see, you had to tap into darkness to become strong enough to curse me, but I did not. Don't you understand? I am not, nor have I ever been, evil, Mamá. You are. And now you must live the rest of your life knowing the atrocities you committed against your very own people."

"Do not do this, Ava," my grandmother hisses, and I glance at her.

No longer by the sliding doors, Abuela is lying on the ground, crawling toward me. She digs her hands into the frozen snow, trying to pull herself upright. I do not aid her.

Her skin is still blanketed in fine, black veins, and I know the darkness still consumes her soul. When I tapped into their magic, I did not grasp on to the evil that resides there.

I know my grandmother is too far gone to save, but I do not know how much time she has left. I hope she will find peace in her final moments, because I want her to pass with clarity. I want her to recognize her downfall was her doing.

"Don't do what?" I ask. "Don't force you to live as an

empty shell? It is too late for begging, Abuela. The spell has been cast, and I will *never* tell you how to reverse it."

"*¡Por favor!*" Mamá screams, but her pain only infuriates me more. How *dare* she ask for mercy after all she has done?

"It did not have to be this way, Mamá," I remind her. "I wanted peace, and now I have it. You see, I can live with what I have done. But can you?"

I turn, ignoring her pleas. I do not listen to the witches who cry, and I do not look back to offer a final glance at my fallen friend. I simply walk away, hand in hand, allies surrounding me as we fade into the shadows.

And I never look back.

ALSO BY DANIELLE ROSE

DARKHAVEN SAGA

Dark Secret

Dark Magic

Dark Promise

Dark Spell

Dark Curse

PIECES OF ME DUET

Lies We Keep

Truth We Bear

For a full list of Danielle's other titles,
visit her at DRoseAuthor.com

ACKNOWLEDGMENTS

With each new book, I confess my admiration for the team behind my career. From my amazing publisher to my readers to my family, so many have played a role in my publishing journey. I would be nowhere without these people, and I worry they will never truly know how much I appreciate their support.

To Heather — Our friendship means so much to me. You are the kindest person I have ever met, and that alone makes me want to be a better person. But then you went and made me a better writer by offering unwavering support and untold wisdom. From pondering plot lines to creating entirely new stories, we always seem to be in sync—like the boy band, but better. I hope you know how much I appreciate you.

To Shawna, Francie, and Robin — You ladies are my cohort. You're there when I need to vent or ask for help or work through writer's block. I love you.

To my family and my readers — You have changed my life. A writer is nothing without a support system, and I couldn't do this job without you all by my side. From questioning early drafts to eagerly devouring advance editions, you are always there to cheer me on. Thank you.

To Waterhouse Press — You are an incredible bunch of people, and I am so honored to be part of the family. Thank you so much for giving me a chance.

ABOUT DANIELLE ROSE

Dubbed a "triple threat" by readers, Danielle Rose dabbles in many genres, including urban fantasy, suspense, and romance. The *USA Today* bestselling author holds a master of fine arts in creative writing from the University of Southern Maine.

Danielle is a self-professed sufferer of 'philes and an Oxford comma enthusiast. She prefers solitude to crowds, animals to people, four seasons to hellfire, nature to cities, and traveling as often as she breathes.

Visit her at DRoseAuthor.com

CONTINUE READING
THE DARKHAVEN SAGA